WHAT'S HIS

(A Peyton Risk Suspense Thriller —Book 1)

Ella Swift

Ella Swift

Ella Swift is author of the PEYTON RISK mystery series, comprising five books (and counting).

An avid reader and lifelong fan of the mystery and thriller genres, Ella loves to hear from you, so please feel free to visit ellaswiftauthor.com to learn more and stay in touch.

ISBN: 978-1-0943-8371-2

BOOKS BY ELLA SWIFT

PEYTON RISK MYSTERY SERIES

WHAT'S HIS (Book #1)
WHAT'S LEFT (Book #2)
WHAT'S WISHED (Book #3)
WHAT'S GONE (Book #4)
WHAT'S MINE (Book #5)

PROLOGUE

Elisabeth Hall was so lost in thought as she walked along the forest trail that she almost didn't hear the sound of the rattler. When the sound did register in her mind, she froze suddenly, not daring to move an inch.

Her heart pounded in her chest as she scanned her surroundings—tall, ancient trees stretched toward the sky while vibrant green ferns and underbrush filled the spaces between their trunks.

Where is it? she wondered.

Elisabeth had been hiking in Yellowstone for the past week, seeking solace from her busy life and the constant pressure of being Senator Joseph Hall's daughter. She yearned for something more than the American Dream, feeling that life was too short to waste on material pursuits like a big house, a three-car garage, or an early retirement. She had always been a visionary, seeking adventure and meaning beyond the confines of wealth and status. With every step she took deeper into nature, she felt more determined to make the most out of her life.

"Okay, stay calm," she whispered to herself, straining her ears for any sign of the snake's location. The eerie quiet of the woods only amplified her own breathing and heartbeat in her ears. As the daughter of a prominent politician, Elisabeth had been taught to remain poised and composed in the face of adversity, but this situation was unlike any she had faced before.

Her thoughts drifted back to a conversation she'd had with a trail guide earlier in her journey. He had mentioned the various snakes native to Yellowstone, some poisonous, others harmless. She tried to recall the details, but her mind was a whirlwind of fear and confusion.

"Why didn't I pay more attention?" she muttered under her breath, desperately trying to remember which snakes posed a threat. Her gaze darted from one shadowy patch of underbrush to another. Sunlight filtered through the dense canopy above, casting dappled patterns onto the forest floor. The haunting rattle echoed in her ears, not unlike the ticking of a clock, reminding her that every second counted.

"Focus, Elisabeth," she whispered to herself, trying to recall the conversation she had with the trail guide. He had been eager to share his knowledge, detailing the various species of snakes that called Yellowstone home. "There are only two venomous species here: the prairie rattlesnake and the western rattlesnake," he had said. "They tend to stick to dry, rocky areas—places where they can easily bask in the sun or hide beneath rocks."

As Elisabeth scanned her surroundings, she noticed the terrain didn't particularly match the description the trail guide had given her. Still, did that mean it was impossible to find a rattlesnake here?

Taking a deep breath, she tried to focus her thoughts and remember any other details the guide had shared.

"Both of these rattlesnakes have triangular heads, elliptical pupils, and heat-sensing pits between their eyes and nostrils," he'd said. He had also mentioned something about their coloration, but those details were frustratingly elusive.

Unable to locate the snake, Elisabeth hesitated, wondering if it had simply moved on. Her chest tightened as she debated whether or not to risk taking another step. Finally, she steeled herself and lifted her foot, feeling a surge of adrenaline.

Please, don't let the snake be there, she thought, praying for a reprieve.

But fate had other plans. As her foot hit the ground, she finally spotted the snake, coiled and ready to strike. Its fangs pierced her leg just above the ankle, and she gasped in pain. In an instant, the snake darted away, its sinuous body melting into the underbrush like a wraith.

"Wait!" Elisabeth cried, desperate to get a better look at the creature that held her fate in its venomous bite. But it was too late—the snake had vanished, leaving her with nothing but a throbbing wound and a racing heart.

"Was it one of them? Was it poisonous?" she wondered, panic clawing at the edges of her thoughts. She knew she needed answers, but first, she would have to survive long enough to find them.

She limped to a nearby rock, wincing with every step. Her breath came in short, shallow gasps. The vibrant green foliage around her seemed to blur together as she tried to focus on her wounded ankle.

"Alright, Elisabeth, just breathe," she whispered to herself, sitting down on the rock and carefully peeling back her sock to examine the bite. Two small puncture marks oozed blood, surrounded by an angry red halo. "It's probably not poisonous... right?" She tried to sound confident, but her voice trembled, betraying her anxiety.

Struggling to remember what the trail guide had told her about the park's snakes, Elisabeth frowned, frustration mounting as the details remained stubbornly hazy. "Weren't there only two poisonous species?" she muttered, wracking her brain for any scrap of information that might help her.

Suddenly, the obvious truth clicked: *all* rattlesnakes were poisonous. A chill ran down her spine as she recalled the unmistakable rattling sound that had alerted her to the snake's presence.

"Okay, okay," she said, her voice tense and shaking. "I need help." She fumbled in her pocket for her phone, her fingers slick with sweat. Turning it on, she stood precariously on the rock, holding the device high above her head, praying for a signal.

"Come on, come on," she urged, her eyes darting between the screen and her surroundings. The bars remained stubbornly empty. Elisabeth felt a hysterical laugh bubble up in her chest. The one time she truly succeeded in escaping civilization, and it might just be the death of her.

"You've got to be kidding me," she muttered, the irony bitter on her tongue.

Her hand tightened around the phone, knuckles turning white as she fought to suppress the rising panic. *I can't just sit here and do nothing,* she thought, her mind racing through possible courses of action. The wilderness around her seemed to close in, suffocating her with its oppressive silence.

She closed her eyes, forcing herself to take slow, deep breaths. "Inhale through the nose, exhale through the mouth," she told herself, remembering a technique she'd learned years ago during an anxiety-ridden semester in college. Gradually, her breathing steadied, and she felt the icy grip of fear begin to loosen its hold.

Desperate for a plan, she rummaged through her backpack until her fingers closed around the crumpled map she had stuffed inside earlier. Her hands trembled as she smoothed it out on her lap, scanning the landscape marked with trails, mountains, and rivers. "There's got to be someplace nearby."

Her finger traced the path she had been following, stopping when she found what she was looking for—a lodge just a few miles down the trail. "That's it," she whispered, hope flickering within her. "If I can make it there, someone will be able to help."

Clutching the map, she carefully folded it back up and slid it into her pocket. Then, with renewed determination, she pushed herself off the rock and began making her way along the trail. The setting sun cast long shadows across the forest floor, dappling the earth with patches of light and dark. Tall pines stood sentinel around her, their branches swaying gently in the breeze.

As Elisabeth hiked deeper into the woods, the silence grew more profound—no birds chirped overhead, no squirrels chattered from the trees. It was as if the entire world held its breath, watching her. Despite the comfort of knowing she had a destination, the isolation weighed heavily on her, a reminder of how vulnerable she was in this vast, untamed wilderness.

Her ankle throbbed with each step, the pain a cruel counterpoint to the beauty of her surroundings. She clenched her teeth, determined not to let it slow her down. "I can't stop," she repeated like a mantra, willing herself to keep moving forward.

The path grew increasingly dense with vegetation, making it difficult for Elisabeth to navigate. The bushes that flanked her were a tangle of wild roses and mountain holly, their thorny branches scratching at her exposed skin as she pushed through them. Beads of blood welled up on her arms and legs, but she couldn't afford to slow down.

A sudden snap cut through the undergrowth, freezing Elisabeth in her tracks. Her breath caught in her throat, and she strained her ears for any further sounds. It had been too loud for a small animal—more like a branch cracking beneath the weight of something heavier.

Her mind raced as she recalled the trail guide's warning about bears foraging in areas with dense berry bushes. She knew she was deep in bear country now.

"Hello?" she called out hesitantly, her voice shaky. "Is anyone there?"

No response came, leaving her feeling even more vulnerable than before. She took a deep breath and continued onward, her heart pounding against her chest. With every step, the rustling of nearby foliage intensified, accompanied by heavy footfalls. Elisabeth felt her chest tighten; the oppressive vegetation seemed to be closing in around her, trapping her.

"Hey!" she shouted, trying to startle any bears that might be lurking nearby. "I'm here! Don't come any closer!"

Still, nothing happened. She swallowed hard, fighting back the rising tide of panic within her. She forced herself to keep moving, despite the relentless assault from the thorny bushes and the ominous footsteps that seemed to grow louder with each passing moment.

Suddenly, her heart leaped with hope as she spotted a clearing up ahead. Convinced that a bear was hot on her heels, she mustered all her strength and sprinted to escape the suffocating bushes. She burst through the barrier of thorny branches, gasping for air as she spun around to confront her pursuer.

But there was nothing there. No snarling beast, no vicious predator—only the eerie silence of the forest. Elisabeth's chest heaved as she tried to catch her breath, her mind racing. Could it be that the bear had given up? A small smile of relief crossed her face, and she allowed herself a moment to savor her apparent victory.

"Maybe my luck is turning," she whispered to herself, the optimism that defined her personality beginning to shine through once again.

With renewed determination, Elisabeth turned to resume her journey toward the lodge. Up ahead, she saw a small grove of trees—their gnarled trunks twisted together, their leaves casting dappled shadows upon the ground.

As she neared them, something about one of the trees caught her eye, making her hesitate.

"Wait a minute...what's wrong with that tree?" she murmured, squinting in an attempt to see more clearly.

The longer she stared at the misshapen tree, the more uneasy she felt. It was as though it was watching her, its form not quite right. And then, suddenly, she realized why: a pair of eyes was staring back at her from within the strange contours of the tree.

Her heart dropped like a stone in her chest, and she watched, paralyzed with terror, as a man in a ghillie suit detached himself from the bark. His movements were smooth and silent, his predatory gaze never leaving hers.

Pure terror coursed through Elisabeth's veins as she whirled around and took off running, her heart pounding in her chest like a relentless drum. Her breath came in ragged gasps, the sound of her own fear echoing in her ears. She dared to glance over her shoulder, her eyes wide with panic, and spotted the man in the ghillie suit advancing on her.

"Stay away from me!" she shouted, her voice shaking as adrenaline surged within her. But her warning went unheeded; the man continued to close the distance between them.

Elisabeth's injured ankle throbbed with every step she took, but she pushed herself to keep moving, ignoring the pain. She could feel the cold sweat beginning to bead along her forehead, making her hair cling to her skin.

Please, let this be a nightmare, she thought, praying that she would wake up any moment now, safe and sound in her tent.

The ground beneath her feet seemed to betray her as she tripped, her injured ankle giving out under the strain. Elisabeth hit the ground hard, feeling the scrape of rocks and dirt against her palms. She rolled onto her back, her chest heaving as she sucked in air, trying to gather her wits.

Get up, get up, get up! she urged herself, her mind racing with thoughts of escape. She had to find a way to survive this, to make it back to her family and the life she'd left behind.

But before she could act on her desperate plan, the man loomed above her, his ghillie suit casting an eerie shadow across her face.

"Going somewhere?" he asked.

Elisabeth screamed, and the man's hand reached for her throat, his fingers tightening like the talons of a bird of prey.

CHAPTER ONE

The heavy steel door groaned as FBI Agent Peyton Risk pushed it open, stepping out onto a rooftop with her gun drawn. A gust of wind tousled her dark, chestnut-brown hair, carrying the scent of rain and exhaust fumes from the streets below. The city was alive with pulsating energy, a symphony of traffic and voices reverberating through the night air.

Chicago's skyline spread out before her, a glittering panorama of glass and steel monuments disappearing into the inky darkness overhead. She found herself on top of an old brick building, one that stood out among the modern skyscrapers like a defiant relic of the past. The rooftop was cluttered with debris—discarded cigarette butts, crumbling bricks, and rusted machinery long forgotten.

"Where are you, Ward?" she muttered to herself as her hazel eyes scoured the darkness behind an air conditioning unit. "You can't hide forever."

Brendan Ward had eluded her grasp for months. A notorious arms dealer and murderer, his criminal empire had left a trail of blood and suffering throughout the city. Peyton knew that catching him was vital, not only to bring justice to his victims but also to prevent the countless others who would suffer if he remained free.

"Give it up, Ward!" she called out across the expanse of the rooftop. "There's nowhere left for you to run!"

Her heart pounded in her chest, adrenaline coursing through her veins as she listened for any response. Silence hung heavy in the air, broken only by the distant hum of traffic far below and the soft rustle of fabric as she moved cautiously across the rooftop.

She noticed a large ventilation shaft partially obscured by shadows. It seemed like the perfect place for Ward to be hiding. Taking a deep breath to steady herself, Peyton crept closer, gun raised and ready to fire.

"Got you now," she whispered as she rounded the corner of the shaft, prepared to apprehend the fugitive.

But there was nothing there. No sign of Ward, just the empty darkness of the night.

"Damn it," she cursed under her breath, frustration mounting as she realized she'd been wrong.

Suddenly, a strong arm wrapped around her waist, lifting her off her feet as another hand covered her mouth, muffling her shocked gasp. Ward had been hiding in plain sight, using a cleverly placed tarp to blend into the background.

"Missed me, didn't you?" he taunted, his voice a sinister whisper in her ear as they struggled for control.

Gritting her teeth, Peyton fought to maintain her grip on the weapon as Ward tried to wrest it from her grasp. His fingers were cold and clammy, like a snake wrapping itself around her hand. She twisted around to face him, and their eyes locked in a battle of wills, each determined not to break.

"Did you really think you could catch me so easily?" he sneered, his breath hot and foul against her face. "You're out of your league."

As his taunts filled her ears, anger surged through Peyton, drowning out the fear that had been gnawing at her. This man had caused too much pain, hurt too many people, and she would be damned if she let him slip away again. Summoning all her strength, she drove her knee upward, connecting with his groin.

Ward's eyes widened in shock and pain, giving Peyton the opening she needed. She shoved him off her with a burst of adrenaline-fueled power, sending him sprawling onto the rooftop.

"Enough!" she shouted, rising to her feet and pointing her gun at the fallen criminal. He lay there, grimacing in pain, just inches from the edge of the rooftop. "It's over, Ward. Surrender now."

Wind whipped around them, carrying the sounds of traffic and the distant hum of city life. The bright lights of the metropolis stretched out before them like a sea of stars, illuminating the countless rooftops below. It was a breathtaking view, but one that only served to remind Peyton of the risk they both faced, teetering on the brink of disaster.

Ignoring her command, Ward slowly pushed himself up, turning his back on her as he faced the abyss beyond the edge of the rooftop. Peyton's heart thudded in her chest, the tension between them palpable. She couldn't afford to hesitate, not when so much was at stake.

"Turn around, Ward," she demanded, her voice wavering slightly as she fought to keep it steady. "Hands on your head. Don't make this any harder than it has to be."

"Harder?" He laughed bitterly, glancing back over his shoulder at her. "This is just the beginning. You haven't seen anything yet."

Peyton's heart raced as she watched Ward approach the edge of the rooftop, his disdain for her commands evident in every step. A chilling gust of wind sent shivers down her spine and ruffled her dark hair.

"Damn it, Ward," she said, her voice desperate, "kneel down and put your hands on your head! You don't have to do this."

"You still don't get it, do you?" he replied, his voice carrying a tone of melancholic amusement. "Life is short, and it's meant to be lived on the edge. Taking risks, pushing boundaries—that's what makes us feel alive."

"Enough with the philosophy," Peyton snapped, trying to keep her frustration in check. "Just kneel, now!"

Ignoring her orders, Ward stepped closer to the edge, peering down into the darkness below. He seemed entranced by the void that awaited him, completely oblivious to the danger he was putting himself in.

"Backup needed at my location," Peyton urgently said into her radio. "Subject is noncompliant and may attempt to jump."

"Copy that, Risk," came the response, tense and efficient. "Hold tight, help is on the way."

"See, life's all about those moments that make your heart race and your blood sing," Ward continued, his eyes locked on the dizzying drop beneath him. "You're feeling it right now, aren't you?"

She said nothing. She was frantically trying to think of a way to reestablish control, to get a handle on this situation before he could do something drastic.

"Tell me, Risk," Ward said, his voice soft and almost hypnotic. "Do you ever wonder what it's like to fly? To let go of everything and just...soar?"

"Stop this!" she shouted, her grip on the gun tightening. "We both know you're not going to jump."

"Ah, but that's where you're wrong." He grinned, his eyes glittering with a dangerous, wild light. "You see, I've been living for moments like this my whole life—and I'm not about to stop now."

"Please, Ward, step back from the edge," Peyton said. She couldn't let him get into her head, but the thought of losing him after all she had gone through was unbearable.

Ward sighed dramatically, as if resigned to his fate, and took a few cautious steps away from the edge. The relief that washed over Peyton was short-lived, however, as he flashed her a mischievous wink.

"Sorry, but I'd rather die a free man than live in a cage," he said, before sprinting toward the edge once more.

"No!" Peyton screamed, her heart pounding out of her chest as she watched helplessly, unable to reach him in time.

Ward leaped into the darkness, disappearing from sight. For one harrowing moment, Peyton feared he had truly ended it all. Her breath caught in her throat as she raced to the edge, peering down into the abyss below.

To her astonishment, however, Ward had landed on a lower rooftop not far beneath them. He had taken the risk, and it had paid off. He now sprinted across the gravelly surface, determined to evade her grasp. The city lights shimmered in the distance, casting an eerie glow on the scene playing out high above the busy streets.

"Damn it!" Peyton cursed under her breath, anger and adrenaline surging through her veins. She would not let him escape justice—not after everything she had sacrificed to bring him to this point.

Realizing Ward would vanish into the urban jungle if she didn't act fast, Peyton gritted her teeth and backed up a few steps. She took off at a sprint, her boots pounding against the gravel of the rooftop. The gap between the buildings loomed before her like a chasm, but fear was not an option. She leaped with everything she had, her stomach rising up into her throat as she soared across the void.

She landed with a thud on the second rooftop, her knees absorbing the impact, sending jolts of pain up her legs. Ignoring the discomfort, Peyton rose to her feet, her eyes immediately scanning for Ward. He was several yards away, weaving through a maze of industrial vents and metal pipes that crisscrossed the roof like a metallic spider's web. The Chicago skyline stretched out around them, a backdrop of twinkling lights and steel giants.

"Stop, Ward! You can't escape!" Peyton shouted. But her words only seemed to spur him on, his pace quickening as he darted toward the next rooftop.

With determination fueling her every step, Peyton gave chase, leaping over obstacles and ducking under low-hanging pipes. Sweat beaded on her forehead, and her breath came in ragged gasps, but she refused to relent. As they ran, the distant *thwump-thwump* of helicopter blades grew louder, signaling backup was finally closing in. There was a good chance, however, that it wouldn't reach them in time.

This was her fight, and hers alone.

The air was thick with the scent of tar and old brick, and the sound of her own panting breaths filled her ears. Ward's retreating figure was silhouetted against the cityscape, a dark shadow against the glimmering lights of the buildings around them.

"Stop, Ward!" Peyton shouted, knowing it was futile but unable to stifle her desperation. "You can't run forever!"

With grim determination, she leaped over a gap between roofs, her heart stuttering in her chest as she narrowly avoided plummeting into the darkness below. As she landed, the impact sent tremors up her legs, but she gritted her teeth and charged forward once more.

Peyton's eyes darted around, searching for an advantage as Ward managed to maintain the distance between them.

"Come on, think," she muttered, cursing herself for being so close and yet so far from apprehending him.

Just as hope began to wane, Peyton spotted her opportunity. The rooftops Ward was following led off in a straight line, but to the left was a higher rooftop, accessible by a metal fire escape clinging to its side. If Peyton climbed up that staircase, she would be able to leap down on the rooftop on the far side, thus ambushing Ward.

Without hesitation, she sprinted toward the rickety staircase, ascending it with surprising speed as every muscle in her body strained with effort.

She reached the top and raced across, pausing at the far end as she waited for Ward to appear.

Any moment now, he should come running along. Any moment now.

Where is he? she wondered as doubt crept in. Had she just made a colossal error? Had she assumed too much—and now lost him?

Then, just when her hope was flagging, she heard the sound of footsteps pounding on the roof below. She peered over the edge and saw Ward racing along the roof, stealing glances over his shoulder. Peyton's heart swelled with hope. She knew she had one chance to catch him, one chance to make things right.

With a deep breath, Peyton launched herself off the rooftop, her body hurtling down toward Ward's path. She saw the shock and fear register on his face as he looked up at her, but before he could react, she had slammed into him with all the force she could muster.

The impact sent them both tumbling to the ground. They grappled for a moment, their limbs tangled and thrashing, but Peyton's determination gave her the edge. She pinned Ward down, her pulse pounding in her temples as she snapped the cuffs around his wrists. "It's over, Ward."

"Risk!" a voice called out from above as several agents rappelled down from the helicopter hovering overhead. They raced toward her, guns drawn and ready for action.

But as they reached Peyton and saw the fugitive already apprehended, their expressions changed from steely focus to admiration. Their weapons lowered as they took in the sight before them: Peyton, breathless but triumphant, with Ward subdued beneath her.

"Good work, Agent Risk," one of the agents said, pride evident in his voice. "Looks like you didn't need backup after all."

CHAPTER TWO

The computer cast a bluish glow on the plain, unmarked cardboard box sitting on Peyton Risk 's desk. She stared at it, puzzled.

What in the world could this be? she wondered.

It was late at night, and only a few dedicated souls were left in the FBI headquarters. None of them met her eyes, and she wondered, with a chill creeping up her spine, how the mysterious package had gotten there.

Peyton had just returned to the office after apprehending Brendan Ward, a dangerous criminal who'd been on their radar for months. She had planned to sit down at her computer and start writing up the report. But the sight of the box had stopped her cold.

Was it a bomb? A threat of some kind?

Her gaze shifted to the agent in the cubicle next to hers. Owen Madrow was a tall, lean man with short-cropped dark hair and a perpetual five o'clock shadow. He wore his usual attire: a crisp white dress shirt rolled up to his elbows, revealing corded forearms. His tie was always slightly askew, giving him a casual air that belied his intensity when working on a case.

Owen seemed to be fiddling with a Rubik's cube, twisting and turning the colorful toy as if trying to solve it. Peyton found this odd because he was ordinarily a hard worker, focused and driven. It was almost like he was just passing the time—which was particularly odd, considering the lateness of the hour.

"Hey, Owen," Peyton said softly, trying to get his attention without alerting the rest of the office.

Owen looked up, his green eyes meeting hers with a hint of surprise. "Peyton! You're back. How did it go with Ward?"

"Caught him," she replied, her voice strained. "But I've got a more pressing issue right now."

She nodded toward the box on her desk. Owen's eyes followed her gaze, and he frowned, his brow creasing with concern. He set aside the Rubik's cube and leaned closer to get a better look at the package.

"Where did that come from?" he asked, his voice low and cautious.

"I don't know," Peyton admitted. "I was hoping you might have seen something."

"Me?" He shrugged innocently. "I've just been studying up on that cyberattack case. I didn't see anyone come in here with a package."

Peyton nodded, though she was not entirely convinced. There was something off about Owen tonight. She couldn't quite put her finger on it, but his demeanor seemed too relaxed, too distracted.

Why wasn't he more curious?

"You sure you didn't see anyone drop this off?" Peyton asked, her eyes narrowing as she observed Owen's demeanor. "Or hear anyone say anything about it?"

Owen shrugged again, his gaze shifting away from hers. "Nope, didn't see a thing. Maybe someone just wanted to surprise you with a gift." He tried to sound casual, but there was an underlying tension in his voice that piqued Peyton's suspicion.

"Really? In the middle of the night?"

"Maybe they didn't want to draw attention," Owen suggested weakly, avoiding eye contact.

Peyton studied him for a moment longer before turning her attention back to the box, her fingers drumming nervously on the edge of her desk. The cardboard seemed innocuous, yet there was something about the situation that set her on edge.

As she pondered over the mysterious package, she considered calling in a bomb squad. But her rational mind reminded her that the box wouldn't have made it past security without being thoroughly checked.

Taking a deep breath, Peyton grabbed a utility knife from her drawer and carefully slid the blade under the tape sealing the box. As she sliced through the adhesive with slow, deliberate movements, she could feel Owen watching her from his cubicle, his presence making her even more uneasy.

The last piece of tape fell away, and Peyton hesitated for a brief second before cautiously lifting the flaps of the box.

Inside the box, Peyton found herself staring at a meticulously crafted cake. Its surface was adorned with an image of an eagle soaring through the sky, its wings spread wide. Upon closer inspection, she realized the face of the eagle was her own, eyes filled with determination and fierceness. Clutched within its talons was a small, helpless creature bearing the unmistakable likeness of Brendan Ward, his face contorted in fear.

"Wow," she muttered under her breath, a smile forming on her lips.

"Pretty impressive, huh?" Owen said, and she turned to see him grinning as he peered into her cubicle. "We figured it's not every day you get to swoop down from a rooftop and snatch up a notorious criminal like some kind of badass eagle."

"Very funny," Peyton said, chuckling as she relaxed. "Who was behind this? You?"

He raised his hands innocently. "It was a group effort. We just thought you could use a little celebration—gotta make the most of the victories you get, right?"

Peyton was about to thank him, but just then the stern voice of Mike Hanson, their boss, cut through the air like a knife.

"Agent Risk, may I have a word?"

Standing in the entrance of her cubicle, he was a tall, imposing man with a perpetually furrowed brow and cold, unsmiling eyes.

"Of course, sir," Peyton said, her smile fading as she glanced at the cake one last time.

"Good luck," Owen murmured under his breath as Peyton followed Hanson, his eyes filled with genuine concern.

With each step toward Hanson's office, Peyton felt a growing unease in the pit of her stomach. Her palms began to sweat, and she wiped them nervously on her pants. She had always sensed that Hanson harbored some sort of grudge against her, but she could never quite put her finger on the reason why. The anticipation of whatever was about to transpire gnawed at her nerves like a ravenous beast.

Hanson left the door to his office slightly ajar as he passed through, revealing a small room that seemed worlds away from the bustling bullpen outside. Taking a deep breath, Peyton pushed the door open and stepped inside, closing it behind her with a soft click.

Hanson's office was an imposing space, dominated by a heavy oak desk and shelves crammed with books on criminal psychology and investigative techniques. A large window offered a view of the city skyline, its lights twinkling in the distance. The air in the room hung heavy, as if weighed down by the gravity of Hanson's authority.

"Sit down," he said tersely, gesturing to the chair opposite him. His face was set in a deep scowl, his eyes radiating a palpable anger that puzzled Peyton.

"Sir, what's the problem?" she asked hesitantly, trying to keep her voice steady. She couldn't help but wonder if her recent success in apprehending Brendan Ward had somehow sparked this confrontation.

"How about you explain to me what in God's name you were thinking?"

Peyton stared at him, completely taken aback by the intensity of his anger. "I...I caught Ward, sir," she stammered, trying to make sense of his outburst. "Isn't that what we wanted?"

"Of course, it is," he said. "But your methods, your reckless disregard for protocol—it's inexcusable."

Her heart raced as she struggled to grasp the implications of his words. She had always been dedicated to her work, and the thought of being reprimanded for her success in capturing a dangerous criminal was both baffling and infuriating.

"Sir, I did everything within my power to bring Ward to justice," she said defensively, clenching her fists in an effort to quell her rising anger. "I don't understand why you're so upset."

"Your wiretap, Risk. You never got the proper authorization from a judge."

Peyton's chest tightened as she realized the severity of the situation. Her jaw set, she attempted to defend herself. "There was no time, sir—a life was at risk. Besides, I *did* file the warrant with the judge. She gave me verbal approval, and I was just waiting for—"

But Hanson cut her off, his voice like ice. "That doesn't change the fact that you disregarded procedure. You've always been a loose cannon, Risk—reckless and unwilling to follow the rules since day one."

Listening in silence, fury roiled within Peyton like a storm brewing on the horizon. She wanted to argue back, to explain how her instincts had saved lives over the years, but she knew it would only fuel Hanson's anger.

"Someone like you," Hanson continued, his gaze drilling into Peyton, "has no place on my team."

Stunned, Peyton could barely find her voice. "Are you firing me, sir?"

"No," he replied coldly. "I'm transferring you. Think of it as...a rehabilitation program."

"Rehabilitation?" she echoed, disbelief etched across her face. "Where are you sending me?"

"You'll be joining a National Parks Service task force." His tone left no room for argument.

As the words sunk in, Peyton felt her world collapse around her. She had dedicated the last five years of her life to the Bureau. Now, in the blink of an eye, everything was changing. And all because of Hanson's relentless vendetta against her.

"Sir, please," Peyton said, desperation creeping into her voice. "I've been nothing but an asset to the Bureau in my time here. I've worked tirelessly and given everything I have to catch criminals and protect innocent people." Her mind flicked through the faces of all the dangerous criminals she'd helped put away.

"Enough," Hanson said, the sharpness in his tone brooking no argument. "My decision is final. Pack your things and be ready to report to the task force first thing tomorrow morning."

She stared at him, her jaw clenched and eyes brimming with a mix of disbelief and anger. Could this really be happening? Surely, this had to be some practical joke played at her expense.

After all, the bottom line was that Brendan Ward, a dangerous criminal, was now in custody. Hanson ought to be celebrating her achievement, not punishing her for it.

Staring at her boss's stony face, however, it was abundantly clear to her that arguing with him would do no good. With no alternatives, she merely nodded and rose, the conversation over.

As she stepped out of Hanson's office, the door closing behind her with an ominous click, the once-muffled sounds of laughter and conversation flooded her senses. The contrast between the somber atmosphere in Hanson's office and the lighthearted banter outside was jarring.

Peyton blinked back tears as she took in the sight of her colleagues gathered around her cubicle, plates of cake in hand. They were laughing and chatting, oblivious to the emotional turmoil consuming her.

"Hey, Peyton," Owen called out, a smile on his face as he held up a plate with a sizable chunk of the eagle-themed cake. "We figured there was plenty to go around, so we helped ourselves. Want a slice?"

She looked at the cake that had once been a symbol of triumph, now tainted by the bitter taste of betrayal. The irony of celebrating her success while her career crumbled around her was too much to bear.

"Thanks, but no," she replied, forcing a tight-lipped smile. "I've lost my appetite."

The words hung in the air as Peyton's heart ached with the knowledge that this would be her last night among them—her team, her friends. With every fiber of her being, she wanted to scream at the injustice of it all.

But she swallowed the bitterness and steeled herself for what lay ahead. Because if there was one thing Peyton Risk knew how to do, it was to face adversity head-on and come out stronger on the other side.

And she'd be damned if she let Mike Hanson take that away from her.

CHAPTER THREE

Peyton stood before the massive stone facade of the National Parks Service headquarters, feeling like a minnow in an ocean of uncertainty. A promising career in the FBI seemed to be slipping through her fingers like sand, and she couldn't help but feel that this was a demotion.

Where will they send me? she wondered. *Will I have to leave Mom's and Dad's cabin, maybe sell it off—despite the years I spent restoring it?* The cabin was in Virginia, near the border with D.C., and thus close enough for Peyton to commute to FBI headquarters. If, with her new job at the NPS, she was assigned to a distant national park, however, she would have no choice but to relocate.

She imagined herself patrolling trails or picking up litter, perhaps even giving guided tours to wide-eyed tourists. As much as she loved the wilderness and parks, it simply didn't compare to the thrill of chasing down criminals or solving complex cases. She envisioned herself planting trees, measuring water quality, and checking campgrounds for fire safety—all important tasks, but seemingly mundane compared to her high-stakes former job.

How had she gotten here?

The D.C. streets bustled around her, the sound of car horns and impatient commuters filling the air. Early morning light cast long shadows across the pavement as the sun peeked over the horizon, bathing the city in a golden glow. Despite the beauty of the scene, the coolness in the air matched the unease growing within her.

Glancing down at her watch, Peyton realized that her meeting was scheduled to begin in just a few minutes. Sighing, she adjusted her jacket and took a deep breath, steeling herself for what lay ahead.

Upon entering the building, Peyton was struck by the scent of fresh pine and earth that filled the air. The sounds of footsteps padding through the polished halls reminded her of a different time, a different place. The walls were adorned with large photographs of breathtaking landscapes from various national parks, each one more stunning than the last. Although the atmosphere was tranquil, it felt entirely foreign to the life she'd built in the FBI.

As she walked deeper into the building, a pair of people passed by in animated conversation. One was a tall man with wavy gray hair, his hands gesticulating expressively as he spoke. Beside him was a younger woman with short-cropped red hair, nodding along intently.

"And the glaciers!" the man was saying with a note of wonder. "It's like being transported to another world entirely. The colors, the textures, it's all so indescribable."

"Leaves its mark on you, doesn't it?" the woman answered, nodding.

As the two moved on and the conversation faded, Peyton couldn't help but feel a pang of envy at their obvious passion for their work. She missed feeling that kind of excitement and drive.

After five years with the FBI, she had come to understand its rhythms, its secrets, and its challenges. She wasn't excited about starting over, but quitting seemed even less appealing. Her career was her entire life, after all. She had almost no friends who weren't colleagues, and she hardly even knew what a hobby was. Quitting – particularly without another job already lined up – would completely demolish the structure of her life, and it frightened her to think what the results would be.

As she continued down the hallway, she spotted a woman walking by. She was middle-aged, with neatly pulled-back dark hair and a kind face that was etched with lines of experience. Her eyes held a steady, confident gaze that seemed to see right through Peyton's uncertainty.

"Excuse me," Peyton said hesitantly, "could you tell me where I can find Peter Marshal? I'm supposed to meet with him."

"Of course," the woman said. "You'll find him in Conference Room B, just down this hall on the left." She gestured in the appropriate direction.

"Thank you," Peyton said, offering a small, grateful smile. As she made her way toward the conference room, she passed more employees, each absorbed in their own tasks or conversations. Their voices mingled with the distant sound of a printer humming and the faint scent of coffee brewing in the break room.

Despite the seemingly mundane activity around her, Peyton couldn't shake the feeling that she was an intruder in this world, a trespasser in a place where she didn't truly belong. But for now, she had no choice but to push forward and meet the man who held the key to her uncertain future.

Her hand hovered over the doorknob as she paused outside Conference Room B. She could hear muffled voices from within, their tones serious and focused. Her heart raced with a mix of nerves and uncertainty, her fingers tingling with anticipation.

"Get it together, Peyton," she muttered to herself, taking a deep breath. Steeling her resolve, she opened the door and stepped inside.

The conference room was spacious, with floor-to-ceiling windows on one side that offered an impressive view of the cityscape beyond. The walls were painted a calming shade of blue, and the air smelled faintly of lemon-scented cleaning products. Dominating the space was a long, polished wooden table surrounded by high-backed leather chairs. A large monitor was mounted on the wall at the head of the table, currently displaying a serene landscape of a national park.

Six people sat around the table, papers and laptops spread out before them. As Peyton entered, a friendly-looking man in a crisp Park Service uniform rose to greet her. His eyes crinkled warmly at the corners, and his salt-and-pepper hair gave him a distinguished air.

"You must be Peyton Risk," he said, extending his hand. "I'm Peter Marshal."

"Nice to meet you, Mr. Marshal," Peyton answered, shaking his hand firmly.

"Please, call me Peter," he said with a smile. "Allow me to introduce you to the rest of the task force." He gestured to the others seated around the table, naming them one by one. "This is Claire, our forensic analyst; Jim, our technology expert; Rosa, who handles logistics and coordination; and finally, Dr. Erica Stevens, our resident biologist."

Each person nodded in turn, offering brief greetings. Then Peter's gaze shifted to a man sitting at the far end of the table who hadn't made any effort to acknowledge her presence. He had a lean, angular face and piercing blue eyes that seemed to evaluate her with an icy detachment. "And this is Sean O'Malley, our wilderness survival specialist."

"Okay," Peyton said, nodding at each of them in turn, though she couldn't help but feel a chill when her eyes met Sean's unwelcoming gaze. Turning back to Peter, she spoke up. "I appreciate the introductions, but I have to admit I'm a bit confused. I've spent years catching criminals, particularly murderers. My skills don't really involve taking care of parks."

Peter looked around the room before addressing her concern. "Well, Peyton, I understand your confusion. But rest assured, your expertise in criminal investigations will be invaluable to us. As you'll come to understand in just a moment, you're here *because* of your background, not in spite of it."

Peyton studied the faces of her new colleagues, trying to gauge their reactions to Peter's words. She wondered what secrets lay beneath their professional exteriors, and whether they shared her own reservations about her sudden transfer to the Park Service. For now, all she could do was trust that she had a role to play in this mysterious task force, and hope that her skills would indeed prove to be an asset.

Peter cleared his throat, commanding the room's attention. "Alright, everyone, let me fill you in on why we're here. This is a high-profile case involving Senator Joseph Hall's daughter, Elisabeth. She was last seen in Yellowstone National Park by a trail guide three days ago."

"How do we know she didn't just get lost?" suggested Rosa, a woman with short-cropped hair and an earnest expression.

"Ordinarily, that would be a plausible theory," Peter said. "However, there have been two other women found murdered in the same area of the park recently: Ernestine Johnson and Leticia Darrow."

The gravity of the situation settled over the room like a heavy fog, and Peyton could feel her heart rate quicken.

Peter clicked a button, and an image appeared on the large monitor. The screen displayed photographs of two smiling women, their eyes bright with life. He continued, "Both of the victims went missing days before they wound up dead, and both were strangled. There were no defensive wounds, which suggests that either the killer knew them or was very skilled at overpowering them."

As Peyton studied the images, her mind began to race, cataloging and evaluating every detail. She couldn't help but wonder if Elisabeth Hall had already suffered the same fate as these two, and they just hadn't found her body yet.

"Time is of the essence," Peter said, as if reading Peyton's thoughts. "If Elisabeth Hall is still alive, she may not have long left. We need to get to Yellowstone and find her as soon as possible."

As the meeting dispersed, Peyton hesitated for a moment before approaching Peter. Her heart thudded in her chest, like a caged bird longing for freedom. The murmurs and shuffles of the task force members leaving the room barely registered as she focused on gathering her thoughts.

"Peter, can I have a word with you?" she asked.

"Of course," Peter replied as he turned to face her.

Peyton took a deep breath, inhaling the lingering scent of stale coffee and musty paper. "I just wanted to be honest with you. I'm not sure what you were told, but I didn't ask to be transferred here—it was forced on me." She glanced down at her hands, feeling the weight of the truth heavy on her shoulders. "The truth is, I have mixed feelings about this. I'm not sure my skills will be best utilized here."

Peter's gaze softened as he listened to her concerns. He leaned in closer, his voice low and steady. "Peyton, your investigative experience is something almost no one else on this task force has. We need you. I understand that this might not be what you envisioned for your career, but I promise you this: after this case, if you still don't want to be here, I'll put in a good word for you. Maybe we can get you transferred somewhere more to your liking. But for now, I need your help."

The sincerity in Peter's eyes stirred something within Peyton—a flicker of hope, perhaps. She felt torn between the familiar allure of her life as an FBI agent and the uncertainty of this new role.

Although she had agreed to help with the case, it occurred to her that she could fight Hanson's decision. She could appeal to someone higher up, show her track record and how much the Bureau needed agents like her. It might be enough to get someone to reverse the decision.

She stared out of the window, the gray skies of Washington D.C. casting a somber veil over the bustling streets below. The city seemed to mirror her own inner turmoil—a constant struggle between duty and desire, loyalty and ambition.

Then, she found herself thinking of her parents and their shared love for the great outdoors. The three of them had spent countless hours exploring the wilderness, marveling at the beauty and grandeur of nature. In those moments, Peyton had felt truly alive, truly free.

All of that, of course, was before her parents had been brutally murdered in Eden's Gate National Park sixteen years ago, when Peyton was only twelve. She remembered little about the day except that her parents had taken a walk together, saying they needed alone time and would return before long to the pond where Peyton was tearing breadcrumbs from her sandwich and tossing them to fish.

They hadn't returned at all, however, and eventually, hearing the wail of sirens in the distance, Peyton had grown troubled and decided to go looking for her parents. She'd encountered a ranger, an older woman who, after Peyton had identified herself, had looked at her with pitying eyes and, placing a comforting hand on Peyton's shoulder, told her the news that would change her life forever.

Only sometime later, while reading about the murders online, had Peyton discovered that her parents had been shot to death. Who had shot them or why, however, remained a complete mystery.

Now, standing in front of Peter Marshal as he waited for an answer, she fingered her necklace, a delicate piece of art her mother had made from sea glass and driftwood, which Peyton had scavenged from a beach when she was a child. She often touched it when she was thinking of her parents.

Maybe this is what I need, she thought, picturing Elisabeth Hall's face. She couldn't bring her parents back, but she could bring this innocent young woman back. It was what her parents would've wanted.

"Alright," she said aloud, her voice resolute. "I'll do it."

Peter smiled. "I was hoping you'd say that. You won't regret this, Peyton—I promise. You're going to do great."

She nodded, appreciating the words even if she didn't really feel them, and turned to go.

Peter's voice stopped her. "There's one more thing, Peyton." He paused, his gaze fixed on her. "We typically have our rangers work in pairs, so you'll be teamed up with Sean O'Malley."

Her heart sank like a stone in water. Sean O'Malley was the last person she wanted to work with, giving the cold attitude he'd displayed during the meeting. But she knew that there was no time to waste, no room for hesitation or doubt. And so, summoning every ounce of strength that she could muster, she gave a curt nod and strode toward the door.

It'll be fine, she told herself. *I can handle him.*

As she stepped out into the corridor, her mind raced with a thousand questions, each one more pressing than the last. What would she discover on this new journey? How would she navigate having a new partner?

And, most importantly, could she save Elisabeth Hall in time?

Only one thing was certain: there was no turning back now. The die had been cast, and she was about to embark on the adventure of a lifetime.

CHAPTER FOUR

Charon traced his fingers across the bear's fur, marveling at its velvety softness. He felt a strange kinship with these powerful creatures, an innate understanding of their instincts and prowess. They were both mighty hunters, stalking their prey with cunning and patience, and they shared a fierce independence that was unrivaled in the natural world. Charon admired the bear's ability to be both gentle and ferocious, a duality that he himself possessed.

As the morning sunlight filtered through the treetops, casting dappled shadows on the ground below, Charon studied the bear hide, which was stretched taut on a homemade frame. He had constructed the frame using only primitive tools, a practice he adhered to for all his projects. It taught him greater self-reliance, pushing him to be resourceful and resilient in a modern world that often favored convenience over integrity. Furthermore, Charon believed it was more respectful to the earth to use the materials it provided naturally, rather than exploiting its resources for mass-produced, disposable items.

The frame, built from sturdy branches and lashed together with sinew, showcased Charon's skill and determination. Each joint had been meticulously carved and secured, ensuring the integrity of the structure despite its seemingly rudimentary design. The bear hide itself bore testimony to the precision and care with which it had been removed from its original host, a testament to Charon's respect for the animal that had given its life.

"Your spirit lives on," Charon whispered to the hide, his eyes glinting with gratitude. "You are now part of something greater."

In his heart, Charon knew that his connection with nature transcended that of most people. Through his primitive practices, he bridged the gap between man and beast, achieving a deeper understanding of the delicate balance that sustained the world around him.

The secluded area in Yellowstone where Charon had chosen to set up his camp was high above the valleys, granting him a panoramic view of the wild landscape below. As the sun climbed higher in the sky, it cast a warm golden light on the verdant forest and rocky outcrops that surrounded him. He breathed in deeply, savoring the crisp mountain air that filled his lungs with a sense of invigoration.

There was a small shack nearby, its weathered wooden walls blending seamlessly into the environment. A headdress adorned with an array of vibrant feathers hung beside the entrance, a symbol of both respect for nature and the prowess of its wearer.

As Charon eyed the bear hide stretched across the frame, he determined it was finally ready. Carefully, he began to detach the hide from the frame, loosening each sinew tie that held it in place. With deliberate precision, he worked his way around the structure, careful not to damage the hide as he freed it from its temporary confines. Once it was completely detached, he lifted the heavy fur and draped it over his shoulders, enjoying the weight and warmth that enveloped him. It felt like a fitting reward for his efforts and a sign of his kinship with the mighty bear.

"Beautiful, isn't it?" he asked rhetorically as he turned toward the young woman crouching inside a wooden cage nearby. Her eyes were wide, and her face pale as she stared at him wordlessly.

"Come now," Charon pressed, a hint of impatience in his voice. "Surely you can appreciate the beauty of nature's finest creations."

Her lips parted slightly, but no sound emerged. Instead, she shook her head minutely, all semblance of defiance drained from her features. Charon couldn't help but feel a twinge of disappointment—he had hoped she might show more spirit.

"Your silence won't change anything, you know," he said, his voice softening. "Embrace this moment, for it is part of a greater purpose."

The woman's eyes flickered with something akin to fear, but she remained mute.

Bored by the woman, Charon turned his attention to the cage, which he had constructed himself. He was proud of his work. Each log had been carefully selected, stripped of its bark, and notched to fit snugly together, creating an inescapable prison for his captive. The craftsmanship spoke to his determination and patience, traits that had served him well in his pursuit of a higher calling.

"Are you afraid of me?" Charon asked, amusement lacing his words as he watched her cower before him.

"What are you going to do with me?" she whispered.

"Ah," Charon mused, tilting his head thoughtfully. "You will serve a great purpose, my dear. One that few could ever hope to achieve."

Her breath hitched, and she clenched her fists tightly, her nails digging into her palms. "My father is Senator Joseph Hall," she said. "He can get you anything you want, just let me go."

Charon couldn't help but smile at her futile attempt to bargain for her freedom. "All I want is to fulfill my destiny, and for that, I need you."

Are you going to kill me, then?"

"Kill you?" He paused, frowning. "Such an ugly word. "Think of yourself as a gift. The earth requires a sacrifice to maintain balance...and that's where you come in."

"So I'm being given to...the earth?" she asked, her voice barely audible.

"To Mother Nature herself," Charon said, his expression one of reverence. "She will embrace you, and bless the land in return."

The woman said nothing. Tired of talking, Charon turned away from her and tried to quiet his mind. He needed to attune himself with the earth before making the sacrifice.

Closing his eyes, he took several deep breaths, allowing the crisp mountain air to fill his lungs, reminding him of his purpose. He focused on the sounds of nature around him: the rustling leaves, the distant trickle of water, and the gentle hum of insects. Every life form was interconnected, all part of a greater whole; he knew that in order to perform this ritual, he had to be at one with the energies of the earth.

"Excuse me," the woman suddenly said, interrupting his meditation. "I need to go to the bathroom."

Charon's eyes snapped open, annoyance flashing across his features. "Just pee in the corner," he snapped.

"Please," she said, her tone pleading. "It'll be a mess. Do you really want me to pee all over the cage and myself? It'll stink."

Frustrated, Charon walked over to the wooden cage. The intricate locking mechanism he'd created allowed him to secure the door tightly. He couldn't help but admire his craftsmanship as he began carefully undoing the various knots and bolts holding the door shut. After all, he had put much thought into designing and constructing the cage, ensuring it would withstand any attempts at escape.

A glint of hope shimmered in the woman's eyes as Charon worked to unlock the cage. He noticed her gaze and paused, tilting his head thoughtfully. "You know," he said conversationally, "I never told you how I killed that bear."

She didn't answer, but her eyes widened slightly, betraying her fear. He smiled, relishing her reaction. "I hunted it with a spear," he began. "I waited for hours, hidden among the trees, my senses attuned to every sound, every movement. And when the bear finally came lumbering into my trap, I struck."

He waited, but she said nothing.

"Like lightning," he continued, "I emerged from the shadows, ambushing the beast. It reared up on its hind legs, roaring its defiance, but it was no match for me. I stabbed it over and over, each thrust of my spear a testament to my mastery over nature. The blood flowed like rivers, staining the earth and feeding its life force." As he spoke, Charon could see the color draining from the woman's face, leaving her pale and shaken.

Charon leaned in close, his breath hot against her cheek. "And just so you know, I still have that spear."

Her voice was as ephemeral as a half-forgotten dream. "I won't try running away."

"Good," he said, nodding, and opened the door to the cage. She hesitated for a moment before stepping out, her movements slow and cautious. She walked toward some blueberry bushes nearby.

"That's far enough," Charon said. "You can do your business there."

"Could you at least look away?" she said. "Give me that much dignity?"

He hesitated, considering. *She won't run,* he thought. *She's cowed, broken. She'll do as she's told.*

"As you wish," he said, turning his back to her and focusing his attention on the surrounding landscape. He could smell the earthy scent of damp soil and decaying leaves, feel the crisp mountain air against his skin. It really was a perfect day.

As he waited, the woman's voice broke through his thoughts.

"I thought you loved nature,' she said, her voice sounding just a bit more confident than before.

He was puzzled by the implication. "I do."

"Then how could you have killed that bear so brutally?"

Charon looked down at the ground, his eyes tracing the delicate patterns of light and shadow formed by the leaves above. He considered her question before answering, his tone calm and resolute. "Killing is nature. It's the cycle of life and death that sustains us all. The bear lived free and wild, and when I killed it, I did so with honor—using my own strength and skill."

He paused for a moment, allowing the words to sink in. "There is no greater respect I could have shown the bear than by making it part of something greater than itself. All of nature is interconnected, and death feeds life. In the end, we all return to the Earth from whence we came."

Charon could sense the woman processing his words, but he didn't care whether or not she understood. His connection to the natural world was something deep within him, something that transcended explanation.

"Are you finished?" he asked, growing impatient with the silence.

There was no answer.

Charon turned around and was surprised to discover that the woman had vanished. How had he not heard her? She must have been as quiet as a cat.

He felt a moment of alarm, but then he calmed himself. *She can't get away,* he told himself. *That's why you chose this location—the wilderness is more of a prison than that wooden cage could ever be.*

Setting the bear pelt aside, Charon began to move toward the thick bushes where she had disappeared. "If you come back now, I'll forgive you," he called out through the trees. "There will be no consequences."

Still, there was no response.

Charon stepped into the undergrowth. They were many miles from any form of civilization, and he knew this place better than anyone. The woman stood no chance of escaping him. A thrill coursed through his veins at the thought of the hunt that lay ahead—the ultimate test of skill and cunning between hunter and prey.

"Very well," he murmured to himself, disappearing into the shadows of the forest. "Time to teach this brat a lesson."

CHAPTER FIVE

As Peyton drove into Yellowstone National Park, she was struck by the overwhelming beauty that surrounded her. The afternoon sun bathed the lush landscape in golden light, enhancing the vibrant colors of the park. Stately lodgepole pines stretched skyward, their branches a playground for nimble red squirrels darting among the needles. A group of bison grazed lazily on the verdant grass, their shaggy coats rippling with each slow movement.

"Wow," Peyton said, her eyes wide with wonder and excitement. A grin spread across her face as she spotted a majestic bald eagle soaring gracefully above the tree line, its powerful wings catching an updraft and carrying it higher into the sky. This place was truly magical, and despite the grim purpose of her visit, she couldn't help but be captivated by the natural splendor before her.

Turning to her passenger, Sean O'Malley, she hoped to share her enthusiasm for the incredible scenery. However, his attention remained focused on his phone, oblivious to the breathtaking view just outside the window.

She studied his face, searching for any hint of emotion or interest. Even during the five-hour flight here from Washington, D.C., he had hardly said a word to her. The distance between them seemed to stretch beyond mere physical space; it was as if he existed in another world entirely.

Peyton furrowed her brow, unsure whether to take his aloof demeanor personally or not. As an FBI agent, she was used to working with various personalities, but there was something about Sean that eluded her understanding. She couldn't help but feel a twinge of curiosity mixed with frustration as she attempted to decipher what lay behind his icy blue eyes.

"Hey, are you seeing this?" she asked, attempting to draw his attention to their surroundings. "Look at those bison! Incredible, right?"

Sean glanced up from his phone, his expression unreadable. "Yeah, it's nice," he replied flatly, before returning his gaze to the screen.

"Nice?" Peyton asked, her voice laced with disbelief. She couldn't comprehend how anyone could be so indifferent to the awe-inspiring beauty that enveloped them. But then again, she reminded herself, they were here for a purpose – a grim one at that – and perhaps Sean was simply maintaining a professional demeanor.

Determined to break the silence, Peyton took a deep breath and decided to try drawing Sean out of his shell. "So, how did you become a wilderness survival expert?"

"Always liked the outdoors," he said, still not looking up from the screen.

"Did you grow up in a place like this?" Peyton pressed, hoping to get more than a few words out of him.

"Montana. Lots of outdoor activities," was all Sean offered before returning to his phone with an air of finality.

Peyton frowned, feeling discouraged by his terse responses and lack of engagement. She tried to remind herself that they were here for a serious reason, but it was hard not to feel slighted by his aloofness.

She decided to make one more attempt. She turned on the radio, then navigated to a folk rock station. Folk music was one of her favorite kinds of music—she loved the simplicity of it, the stories, the focus on nature and living close to the earth and remembering one's roots.

"What kind of music do you like?" she asked Sean as a banjo picked out a series of notes.

"Not this."

Peyton clenched her jaw, frustrated. She jabbed the stereo, turning off the music.

She made no attempt to hide her irritation. "What's so interesting on your phone? You've barely looked up since we got here."

"Sorry if I'm not gawking at the scenery like a tourist," he said, finally locking eyes with her. "I'm reading about the victims—Ernestine Johnson and Leticia Darrow. Seems a bit more important to me than admiring the view."

His words stung her, and she could feel a flush creeping up her cheeks. She knew they weren't here for leisure, but she couldn't help but feel hurt by his blunt dismissal of her appreciation for the park's beauty. It was true they were not tourists, but did that mean they had to ignore the magnificence around them? All she wanted was to connect with her partner, to make their working relationship more bearable.

The air inside the car grew heavy with tension, and Peyton found herself seeking a brief escape. Her phone buzzed in the cup holder, causing her to glance down at the screen. A new text message from

Saul Guzman, her foster father, appeared. Steering the vehicle with one hand, she carefully picked up the phone to read the message.

Hey kiddo, haven't heard from you in a while. Everything okay? – Saul

Peyton's heart swelled with gratitude; even though they didn't share blood, Saul had always been there for her. After her parents' sudden and mysterious murder when she was twelve, Peyton had been kicked around the foster system, never feeling like she truly belonged anywhere. But Saul had taken her in when she was sixteen and had given her a stable home, a sense of belonging, and unwavering love. It was because of him that she had found the strength to become an FBI agent and make a difference in the world.

She remembered how he'd encouraged her during her first few months at the FBI Academy, telling her that he knew she was destined to do great things. He'd believed in her when no one else did, and it was his unwavering support that had propelled her to where she was today.

Taking a deep breath, Peyton typed out a quick response. *Hey Saul! Things are busy, but I'm alright. Got a lot to talk about. I'll call you soon, promise.*

She hit send and placed the phone back in the cup holder, refocusing on the road ahead as the GPS announced their arrival. The dirt parking lot came into view, surrounded by towering pines and the distant sounds of rustling leaves. A wooden sign marked the trailhead nearby, leading deeper into the wilderness. As she parked the vehicle, Peyton realized this must be the path to the second crime scene.

"Looks like we're here," she said, unbuckling her seatbelt and stepping out of the car. The summer breeze brushed against her face, carrying the scent of damp earth and pine needles. She took a moment to appreciate the serenity of the forest before her, knowing that the gruesome scene they were about to investigate would soon shatter it.

"Finally," Sean muttered behind her, slamming the car door shut. His tone was still frosty, but she refused to let it get under her skin.

No matter how hard she tried to focus on her surroundings, however, it seemed impossible not to take Sean's aloofness personally. It was as if he thought she was just another rookie agent tagging along for the ride. She remembered the respect she'd earned from her colleagues back at the Bureau, and it stung to be treated so coldly by someone she was supposed to work closely with.

"Look," she began, deciding to be direct, "I don't know what your problem is with me, but we're here to solve a case. So, let's put our differences aside and get our heads in the game. Okay?"

Sean glanced at her, looking unimpressed. He had to be six feet tall, which gave him a significant six-inch advantage over Peyton.

Sean didn't respond right away. Instead, he kept walking, eyes scanning the surrounding forest as if searching for something. Finally, he spoke up. "I won't get in your way if you don't get in mine."

"Fine."

As they continued deeper into Yellowstone, the terrain shifted beneath their feet, trading leaf-covered earth for rocky soil. Trees gave way to expanses of scrubby bushes, while steep inclines and uneven ground tested their agility. The landscape was wild and untamed.

Through the trees, Peyton spotted a plume of vapor rising into the air. Her heart raced, adrenaline pumping through her veins as she imagined a fire blazing nearby.

"Is that smoke?" she asked, pointing in the direction of the column.

"No," Sean replied, his tone matter-of-fact. "It's steam from a vent. There are quite a few of them around here."

His familiarity with the park struck Peyton as intriguing. Could he have spent time here before? Was he hiding something about his past?

Before she could think of how to broach the subject, the steam vent loomed before them like the gaping maw of an ancient, slumbering beast. Wisps of vapor curled around the edges of the fissure, coiling and dissipating into the crisp air. The ground beneath their feet was a patchwork of earth and rock, cracked and groaning under the relentless pressure from below.

"Here it is," Peyton said, her voice nearly lost in the hissing and bubbling of the vent. She glanced at Sean, expecting some kind of reaction, but his expression remained unreadable.

"Right," he replied simply, as if they were discussing something as mundane as office supplies rather than standing on the precipice of a geological marvel—and a crime scene.

Peyton pulled out her phone, swiping through the photos she'd been sent. The images showed a grisly tableau: Leticia Darrow's body, twisted in agony, face-down in the steaming waters of the vent. Her skin was blistered and raw, the result of prolonged exposure to the scalding heat and caustic chemicals that bubbled beneath the surface. It was a horrific way to die, and Peyton found herself shuddering involuntarily as she studied the pictures.

"What a terrible way to die," Sean muttered, breaking the silence that had settled between them. His gaze was fixed on the steam vent, his blue eyes darkened by the weight of the grim task at hand.

Peyton nodded, feeling the knot in her stomach tighten. Sensing a small connection with Sean, she took a deep breath and suggested, "Why don't we fan out and search the area together? We might find something we've missed."

"Sounds good," Sean said, his demeanor still distant, but more cooperative than before.

They split up, each taking a different side of the steam vent to cover more ground. Peyton moved carefully, her eyes scanning the rocky soil and patches of sparse vegetation for any sign of evidence. She tried to push aside the haunting image of the victim from the crime scene photos, focusing instead on the task at hand.

"Found anything?" she called out, her voice carrying through the quiet afternoon air.

"Nothing yet," he said. "What about you?"

Peyton was about to reply in the negative when something caught her eye—a single feather lying partially hidden beneath a scraggly bush. Puzzled, she crouched down to examine it more closely. It was long and slender, with striking black and white markings that she didn't recognize.

"Hey, I found this," she said, holding up the feather for Sean to see. "But it's probably nothing, just from some local bird."

Sean furrowed his brow as he took the feather from her, studying it intently. The troubled expression on his face deepened, and he looked up at her with a mixture of confusion and concern.

"Peyton, this isn't from any bird native to Yellowstone," he said quietly. "It's from a secretary bird—an African species."

"African?" Peyton repeated, puzzled. "Then what the hell is it doing here?"

CHAPTER SIX

"How did you know that feather we found was from a secretary bird?" Peyton asked as she and Sean walked toward Pinecrest Health Center, a modest hospital that served as a critical lifeline for Yellowstone National Park. The exterior of the building was a blend of rustic charm and modern functionality—wooden beams supporting large glass windows, with a sloping roof that seemed to welcome visitors while simultaneously preparing for harsh weather. This was the place where park rangers, tourists, and locals alike would receive treatment for everything from mechanical injuries to rattlesnake bites and bear attacks.

Sean glanced at her sideways, his eyes unreadable beneath furrowed brows. "Just a guess, really," he said.

Peyton raised an eyebrow but decided not to press the issue further. She had learned early on in her career that sometimes it was better to let people keep their secrets, especially when they were still trying to figure each other out. Instead, she changed the subject, hoping to draw him out another way.

"So, how long have you been working for the NPS?"

"About nine years," Sean answered.

Peyton waited for more, but nothing more came. Sean's reticence made her suspect he held something against her, but she couldn't fathom what that might be.

We've never met before, have we? she wondered.

The heavy metal door groaned as Peyton and Sean entered the morgue, its cold sterility a stark contrast to the warm hues of the late afternoon sun outside. A faint scent of disinfectant hung in the air, mingling with the unmistakable odor of death that lingered in the room.

"Welcome," came an unexpectedly cheerful voice, breaking through the oppressive silence. A smiling man stood near a row of gleaming steel tables, his slender frame draped in a white lab coat. He was a peculiar man, thin and wiry despite his age, with a shock of unkempt white hair and a pair of thick-rimmed glasses perched precariously on the bridge of his nose. His bright eyes darted around the room, giving him an air of constant curiosity.

"Dr. Taylor, this is Special Agent Peyton Risk from the FBI," Sean said, gesturing toward her. "She's here to assist with the investigation."

"Former agent," Peyton said, feeling it was important to make this distinction. "I'm with the NPS now."

"Ah, wonderful!" Dr. Taylor exclaimed, extending a gloved hand for a surprisingly firm shake. "I've always found collaborative efforts to be quite stimulating. We'll make a splendid team, my dear."

Despite the morbidity of their surroundings, Peyton couldn't help but feel intrigued by the eccentric doctor. There was something about his enthusiasm and energy that was infectious, even in the face of such grim circumstances.

She turned her attention to the body laid out on the gurney, a young woman no older than thirty with long, dark hair that framed an ashen, almost peaceful face. Her once-vibrant skin had taken on an unnatural pallor, marred by patches of red where the scalding steam had seared through her delicate flesh.

"Leticia Darrow, I presume?" she asked. The first victim, Ernestine Johnson, had already been autopsied, though Peyton and Sean had yet to receive the report.

The coroner nodded, his good-natured expression darkening. "I'm afraid so."

"Such a tragic waste," Peyton murmured softly, her gut twisting with empathy for the victim. "What can you tell us about the effects of the steam on the body, Dr. Taylor?"

"Ah, yes," he replied, adjusting his glasses as he leaned in for a closer examination. "As you can see, the steam caused significant damage to the epidermis and dermis layers, rendering them nearly unrecognizable in some areas. This will undoubtedly make it difficult to find any viable DNA samples that the killer may have left behind."

"Can you confirm the cause of death for both victims?" Sean asked.

Dr. Taylor took a hesitant breath. "I haven't finished the reports – I intend to do a more thorough examination of Ms. Johnson once I've finished the preliminaries with Ms. Darrow here – but I can share my observations. As far as cause of death, it's abundantly clear that both women were strangled." He pointed to Leticia's neck, where faint bruises had formed despite the steam's damage. "You can see the ligature marks here, consistent in both cases."

Peyton's heart sank at the confirmation, and she couldn't help but envision Elisabeth Hall, still alive but perhaps facing the same grim fate.

"Any idea when they were killed?" she asked.

The coroner rubbed his chin thoughtfully. "I'd say they both died about forty-eight hours after they went missing."

"Could be the start of a pattern," Sean said.

As Peyton processed the weight of Sean's words, the door to the morgue suddenly burst open with a loud bang. A man strode in, his face red with anger and authority radiating from every inch of him. Behind him, two stoic men in suits followed, their expressions unreadable but undeniably intimidating.

"Who's in charge here?" the angry man demanded, his voice booming through the sterile room.

Taken aback, Peyton's mind raced as she tried to assess the situation. The man was tall, with salt-and-pepper hair that hinted at a lifetime of determination and power. His suit was impeccably tailored, suggesting wealth and influence. But it was the cold fury in his eyes that commanded her attention.

"Sir, I'm Special Agent Peyton Risk, and this is Ranger Sean O'Malley," she replied cautiously, mentally preparing herself for whatever confrontation might follow. "Can I ask who you are?"

"I'm Senator Joseph Hall," he said. "My daughter has been missing for nearly twenty-four hours, and I've heard nothing about your damn investigation! Nobody's even found the RV she was staying at! What kind of sorry excuses for investigators are you?"

"Sir, we understand your concerns," Peyton said, attempting to mask her own growing anxiety. "But we're doing everything we can. You really shouldn't be here right now."

Hall's gaze shifted to the body on the gurney, his face draining of color. "Is that...is that my daughter?"

"No, it isn't," Peyton quickly reassured him as Dr. Taylor moved to cover the body with a sheet. "As far as we know, Elisabeth is still alive, and we're working tirelessly to locate her."

"Good," he said, his anger momentarily quelled. "You'd better find her. I want answers."

"Senator," Sean said, stepping forward with a calm, steady voice that seemed to fill the room. "I assure you, our top priority is finding Elisabeth safe and sound. We're exhausting every resource at our disposal."

His words were measured and diplomatic, carefully chosen to soothe the senator's frayed nerves without overpromising or downplaying the gravity of the situation. Peyton couldn't help but admire his ability to navigate the delicate balance between empathy and professionalism.

Hall's tense shoulders relaxed ever so slightly, though his eyes remained sharp and guarded. "You need to find her, no matter what it takes," he insisted, his tone softening just enough to hint at the desperate father beneath the veneer of political authority. "Because if you don't, I promise heads will roll."

The sterile scent of disinfectant lingered in the air as Peyton watched Senator Hall's retreating figure, his bodyguards flanking him like ominous shadows. The weight of his words hung heavily in the room. She shook off the unease that crept up her spine, turning to face her new partner.

"What did he mean there at the end?" she asked, searching for any hint of concern in Sean's stoic expression. "Was he threatening us?"

Sean's blue eyes met hers, steady and unwavering. "Does it matter?" he replied, shrugging off the question. "Either way, we're going to do everything we can to find Elisabeth."

Peyton nodded, knowing he was right. Their focus needed to be on the task at hand, not on potential consequences. "If the killer follows the same timeline, then Elisabeth only has about twenty-four hours left," she said, picking up where they'd left off before the interruption. "We should look for the RV the senator mentioned. There might be something there that could help us."

Sean nodded. "Sounds like a plan."

Before they left, Peyton took one last glance at Leticia Darrow's lifeless body, now covered by a crisp white sheet. A shiver ran through her as she noticed something peculiar: an odd discoloration around the victim's wrist. She lifted the sheet slightly, revealing a pattern of faint red lines and smudges encircling the pale skin.

"Look at this," she said, trying to make sense of the markings. As he joined her side, she could see the curiosity flicker in his eyes.

"Ah," Dr. Taylor said. "I was meaning to mention that."

"Looks like transfer from something...maybe rope or fabric," Sean said, studying the reddish imprint. "Could be from when the killer restrained her."

"Or it could be a clue to where he's keeping Elisabeth," Peyton said, her mind racing with possibilities. "We need to analyze this, see if we can learn anything about what made the mark."

"I'm already on it," Dr. Taylor said with a smile.

"Good," Peyton said. "As soon as you learn something, let us know."

With that, she nodded at Sean, and they headed out of the morgue together.

Unspoken between them was an understanding: Elisabeth Hall's life hung by a thread, and they were the only ones who could save her. The clock was ticking, and they had no time to lose.

CHAPTER SEVEN

The tires of the SUV crunched over gravel as Peyton peered through the windshield, her dark brows furrowing in concentration.

"Where is it?" she murmured.

The narrow road they were on was flanked by towering pines, their green needles filtering the afternoon sunlight into shadowy patterns on the ground. She could hear the distant rush of a river, hidden from view by the dense foliage that surrounded them.

"I think we've been here already," she said to Sean, her voice laced with frustration. "We must have gotten turned around somewhere."

Sean shifted in his seat, his fingers tapping on the map he held. "I don't think so. We're close to Elisabeth Hall's RV, according to the directions of the park ranger who last spotted it."

As much as Peyton wanted to believe what Sean was saying, they had been searching for the RV for over an hour now, most of that time spent in the area to which the ranger had directed them. Peyton was beginning to suspect the ranger's memory might not be quite as sharp as he thought.

"Look," she said, pointing to a gnarled tree trunk with distinctive markings. "That's the same tree we passed an hour ago. I remember those claw marks on the bark. Maybe the GPS is leading us in circles."

There was a stubborn edge to Sean's voice as he insisted, "The GPS isn't wrong, Peyton. If we've gone this way twice, it probably just means you missed the turn the first time."

Peyton bristled at the suggestion, her hands tightening on the steering wheel. "Are you saying this is my fault?" she asked, her voice sharp with indignation.

"Take it easy," Sean said, raising an eyebrow. "We're both under a lot of pressure here. I'm just saying we might have overlooked something."

As if on cue, a barely-visible opening appeared in the thick vegetation up ahead, revealing a narrow track that veered off from the main road. Relief washed over Peyton as she realized they had finally found the elusive turn they had been searching for.

"Looks like we found it," she muttered. She gripped the steering wheel tighter and turned the SUV onto the hidden track, their tires crunching over fallen leaves as they ventured deeper into the wilderness.

The camping area was almost eerily quiet, devoid of the usual sounds of excited campers and laughter. Instead, the only noises that broke the silence were the crunching of gravel beneath their tires and the rustling of leaves stirred by a gentle breeze.

"Over there," Peyton said, pointing toward an RV parked at the back of the area, nestled close to the trees. She couldn't help but feel a shiver of anticipation run down her spine as they drove closer.

Pulling up alongside the RV, Peyton shifted the SUV into park, the engine rumbling to a stop. For a moment, she and Sean sat in silence, each lost in their thoughts as they stared at the innocuous-looking vehicle that could hold the key to Elisabeth's fate.

The afternoon sun cast long shadows across the secluded camping area as Peyton and Sean stepped out of their vehicle. The air was cool and crisp, carrying the earthy scent of pine needles and damp soil. Before them stood the RV, its beige exterior blending in with the surrounding wilderness. It appeared to be an older model but in decent shape, with no visible signs of struggle or forced entry.

"Looks like nothing's out of place," Sean said, scanning the area.

"Let's see if we can find anything inside," Peyton replied, her eyes narrowing as she approached the RV's door.

To her surprise, the door swung open easily. Taking a deep breath, Peyton braced herself for what they might find within and stepped inside, followed closely by Sean. The interior of the RV was cozy and well-kept, reflecting Elisabeth's simple and tidy nature. A small dining table sat near the front, adorned with a neatly folded map and a vase of wildflowers. The shelves lining the walls were filled with books on various subjects – everything from classic literature to birdwatching guides – suggesting that Elisabeth enjoyed filling her time with learning and exploration.

"Seems like she took good care of the place," Sean said as he glanced around the RV. His gaze fell upon a leather-bound journal resting on the bedside table, and he picked it up, thumbing through the pages. "This could give us some insight into her thoughts, her routine."

Peyton nodded, her eyes scanning the space for any other potential clues. She noticed a small wooden box tucked away beneath the bed and crouched down to investigate. Pulling the box out and lifting the lid, she found it to be filled with an assortment of postcards and knickknacks—souvenirs from Elisabeth's travels, perhaps, but nothing that seemed particularly useful to their investigation.

"Find anything?" Sean asked, glancing up from the journal.

"Nothing significant. It seems like she led a pretty normal life out here. Anything in that journal?"

"Nothing that seems relevant." He closed the journal with a clap, then set it aside. He sighed.

Peyton gazed around at the neatly organized shelves and drawers. "No signs of a struggle. I think it's safe to say Elisabeth wasn't kidnapped from her RV."

Sean nodded. "And there's no hiking gear left behind, which suggests she was out on a trail when it happened."

"Exactly," Peyton replied, her gaze drawn to the picturesque scenery framed by the RV's windows. She couldn't help but wonder what had drawn Elisabeth to this place and whether she'd ever felt safe in the heart of the wilderness.

Before leaving, she decided to inspect the bathroom for any additional clues. As she opened the mirrored cabinet above the sink, she discovered several pill bottles lined up in neat rows. The labels were worn, but still legible. She squinted at the small print, trying to decipher the names of the medications.

"Prednisone… Azathioprine… What are these for?" she mused aloud.

"Those are immunosuppressants," Sean said from outside the bathroom. "They're used to treat autoimmune diseases, like lupus or rheumatoid arthritis."

Peyton's brow furrowed as memories from her time at the FBI resurfaced. She'd worked a case involving a young woman with lupus, and the medications were all too familiar. "Sounds like Elisabeth was sick," she said. "But if that's true, why wouldn't the senator mention it?"

"Maybe he didn't want to draw any unnecessary attention to his daughter's condition," Sean suggested. "Either way, I'll give him a call and ask."

"Sounds like a plan. I'm going to head outside and look around."

While Sean called the senator, Peyton slipped past him. The afternoon sunlight was bright, but there was a frailness to it, a hint that it would not last forever.

Peyton's eyes scanned the area surrounding the RV, searching for any signs that could lead them closer to Elisabeth. Tall pines towered above her, their branches swaying gently in the breeze, releasing a calming scent of fresh pine into the air. Despite the beauty of the scene, there was an eerie stillness that left her feeling unsettled.

"Focus," she whispered to herself, forcing her attention back to the task at hand. She moved slowly around the RV, her gaze intent on the ground, hunting for tracks or any other clues. Though she didn't believe Elisabeth had been kidnapped here, it was possible the abductor had visited the site.

As she rounded a large tree, she noticed footprints pressed into the soft earth. Her heart thudded in her chest, and she crouched down for a closer look. The prints were well-defined, suggesting they'd been made recently. Beside the tree lay a pile of cigarette butts, smoked down to the filter.

A sickening realization washed over her—someone had been watching Elisabeth from this very spot. The sheer number of cigarette butts suggested they'd been observing her for some time, waiting for the right moment to strike.

"Sean!" she called. "Get over here!"

He emerged from the RV, phone still in hand. "I couldn't get through to the senator," he said, frustration evident in his tone. "Guess I'll just try again later." He lifted his chin in a quick gesture. "What did you find?"

"Footprints and cigarettes," she replied, pointing out her discovery. "Someone was watching the RV. Watching Elisabeth."

Sean crouched down beside her, examining the evidence. He looked up at her, the grudging admiration in his eyes unmistakable. "Nice find. Judging by the number of cigarettes, the kidnapper must've been observing her for quite some time."

"Exactly," Peyton said. "That level of dedication suggests a certain obsessiveness to the killer's personality. They didn't just stumble upon Elisabeth—they stalked her." A shiver ran down her spine as she voiced her thoughts aloud. What kind of monster were they dealing with?

Sean nodded slowly, clearly taking her theory into consideration. But instead of expressing further approval, he pointed out a detail she had missed. "These footprints," he began, tracing the outline of one with a finger. "They're made by a particular type of boot."

Peyton's eyebrows furrowed, and she shifted her gaze between the prints and Sean's face. "What kind of boot?"

"Vibram soles," he answered, a note of caution in his voice. "They're standard issue for rangers here in Yellowstone."

A cold knot formed in the pit of Peyton's stomach. She tried to keep her voice steady as she asked, "Are you suggesting that one of the rangers could be involved in Elisabeth's kidnapping?"

"I'm not jumping to conclusions," Sean replied, standing up and brushing dirt off his hands. "But we can't ignore this evidence. We need to be careful whom we trust."

Peyton stared at the footprints, her thoughts a chaotic whirlwind of fear and disbelief. Could it really be possible that the killer was a park ranger?

Then a new idea, one even more disturbing than the last, hit her: What if they had already met him?

CHAPTER EIGHT

Peyton stared at the trio of rangers congregated outside the station, troubled.

Could one of them be the killer? she wondered.

It was unsettling knowing that the killer could be walking around the park that very moment, dressed as one of the people trained to help those in need while inwardly he was as predatory as a man-hunting bear. It was hard not to view everyone she met with suspicion.

"Ready to head inside?" Sean asked, his abrupt question startling her from her thoughts. His eyes held a hint of curiosity, as if he'd been trying to read her mind.

"Of course," she said, nodding as she tore her gaze away from the rangers. She took a deep breath, preparing herself for the task ahead, and followed Sean toward the ranger station.

The building itself was modest in size but exuded an air of authority, its log-cabin design blending seamlessly into the natural landscape. A worn wooden sign hung above the entrance, proudly displaying "Yellowstone National Park—Razor Tooth Ranger Station" in faded black letters. As they stepped inside, the scent of pine and coffee filled Peyton's nostrils, a comforting aroma.

The interior was a study in organized chaos, maps and photographs adorning the walls, while shelves overflowed with books and manuals covering every aspect of park management and wildlife conservation. A row of desks cluttered with papers, radios, and various pieces of equipment lined one side of the room, a testament to the tireless work of the staff who called this place their office.

Peyton's eyes were drawn to a man seated at one of the cluttered desks. He was in his mid-forties with a stocky build, graying beard, and deep-set eyes that held an air of wisdom and experience beyond his years. The most striking feature, however, was the white neck brace encircling his throat like a rigid collar.

"Dave!" Sean said, a broad smile spreading across his face as he recognized the man. The excitement was mutual; Dave's eyes lit up, and he attempted to rise from his chair, only to wince as his neck protested the movement.

"Sean, it's been too long," Dave replied, his voice strained but warm. "How've you been?"

"Better than you, by the look of it," Sean said, approaching the desk. "What happened to your neck? You get into a wrestling match with a bison or something?"

Dave chuckled, the sound turning into a pained grimace. "Nah, nothing so glamorous. I tripped over my own two feet during a nighttime patrol, stumbled right into a tree stump. Doctor says I'm lucky I didn't break anything, but it's still one hell of a sprain."

"Sounds like quite the adventure," Sean said, trying to suppress a grin.

Peyton cleared her throat, drawing their attention. Sean turned to her and gestured with an open hand. "Peyton, this is Dave Turner, one of Yellowstone's finest. Dave, meet Peyton Risk. She's helping me with a case."

"Nice to meet you, Peyton," Dave said, offering a smile. "So, what do you think of our little slice of paradise here?"

"Yellowstone is beautiful," she said, her mind briefly wandering to the breathtaking landscapes she had seen since arriving. "It's like stepping into another world."

"Beautiful, yes, but it can be dangerous too," Dave said, gesturing to his neck brace. "You've always got to be on your guard around here."

"Anyway," Sean said, shifting gears in the conversation, "we're here because we're investigating a case." He glanced at Peyton for a moment before continuing. "Two people have been killed in the park, and a third has been kidnapped. We have reason to believe it's all the work of the same person."

Dave's eyes widened, his good-natured demeanor momentarily clouded by concern. "Yeah, I heard about that on the radio. Awful stuff. Can't imagine who'd do something like that."

"Actually, that's why we're here," Sean said. "We found some boot prints near Elisabeth Hall's RV—the kind worn by our rangers. We were hoping you could provide us with a roster of everyone working here."

Dave hesitated. "I don't know. That sounds like a policy violation."

"We're only asking for their names," Sean said. "Nothing else. Besides, who would know?" He winked at Dave.

Dave rolled his eyes. Then, with a heavy sigh, he turned in his chair and started rummaging through the papers cluttering his desk. After a few moments, he pulled out a battered notebook, its pages dog-eared and worn. Holding it up, he squinted at the cover before reaching into a drawer to retrieve a pair of reading glasses.

He put on the glasses and studied the notebook for a moment. "Yep, this is the one. Should be the most recent roster." He closed the notebook and passed it to Sean, who handed it off to Peyton.

Peyton's eyes flicked across the page as she studied the names. What was she supposed to be searching for? It wasn't as though she could expect the killer's name to give him away. Any of these people could be their killer.

"We'll just have to interview them one at a time," Sean murmured beside her.

Then Peyton noticed something. "Hey, what's this asterisk next to Frank Petrel's name?" she asked, tapping on the paper with her index finger. She glanced up at Dave, who seemed hesitant to answer.

"Uh, well..." Dave shifted uncomfortably in his seat, obviously not eager to divulge any information. "Frank's on disciplinary leave right now."

"Disciplinary leave?" Peyton raised an eyebrow, her interest piquing. "What did he do?"

"Come on, Dave," Sean said, sensing his friend's reluctance. "We're just trying to get to the bottom of this case. Anything you can tell us might help."

Dave sighed, running a hand through his hair before finally relenting. "Alright, fine. Frank had been...harassing some of the female guests at the park."

"Harassing them how?" Peyton asked.

"Staring, making lewd comments, following them around," Dave explained. "One woman even said he tried to corner her in a secluded area of the park, but she managed to get away."

Peyton clenched her jaw, fury rising within her like a tidal wave. The thought of such behavior happening in a place meant for families to enjoy nature's beauty was sickening. But more than that, it made her think of the victims.

Was there a connection between Frank's harassment and the murders?

"Where can we find Frank?" Sean asked.

Dave hesitated, biting his lip. "He used to live with his mother, but I heard she kicked him out when she found out about the harassment."

"Where is he living now?" Peyton asked.

"I'm not sure," Dave admitted, scratching his head. "But Frank has always been a bit...different. He had this pet project in the park—a cabin he was building using only primitive tools and techniques. He's not supposed to be on park grounds while he's on leave, but knowing Frank, that might not stop him."

"Where is this cabin?" Peyton asked.

Dave slowly rose from his chair, wincing slightly as he did so. He ambled over to a large map that covered almost the entirety of one wall. The map depicted Yellowstone in impressive detail, every contour and landmark meticulously marked. It was clear that this was no ordinary tourist souvenir; it was a tool, a testament to the rangers' intimate knowledge of the land they protected.

"Frank's cabin should be around here," Dave said, pointing to a remote area of the map, far from any marked trails or points of interest. "I only saw it once, but I remember how proud he was of it. He used to go on and on about how modern civilization had lost touch with nature, how we needed to get back to our roots."

Peyton studied the map, the contours and landmarks swimming before her eyes as she tried to make sense of it all. She couldn't help but wonder what kind of man Frank Petrel was—a man who could harass innocent women in one breath, then wax poetic about the beauty of nature in the next. What twisted thoughts lurked behind his facade of rugged individualism?

Sean traced the rugged area on the map, his eyes narrowing as he took in the dense forests and steep slopes. "That terrain looks pretty tough," he remarked, glancing over at Dave. "Can we take ATVs out there?"

"Sure thing," Dave replied. "We have some park vehicles you can use. There's a shed out back." He led them outside, jingling his keys in his hand and tossing them into the air with an easy whistle. The sun cast long shadows across the ground as they approached the shed, its weathered wood blending seamlessly with the surrounding trees.

As Dave unlocked the shed door, the sounds of the forest enveloped them. Peyton couldn't help but feel the weight of the wilderness pressing in on her, reminding her of how small she was in the grand scheme of things.

The shed door swung open, revealing a pair of gleaming ATVs nestled among various tools and equipment. Dave handed each of them a key, the metal cool to the touch.

"Thanks, Dave," Sean said, stepping toward the nearer ATV.

"Before you head off, let me give you a quick rundown on these babies," Dave said, motioning for Peyton to join Sean by the vehicles. As they listened, the familiar hum of machinery mixed with the rustle of leaves in the wind.

"Make sure you've got your helmets on—safety first," Dave began, pointing to a row of helmets hanging along the wall. "Now, starting these up is pretty simple. Just insert the key here," he indicated, pointing to the ignition, "and turn it to the right. You'll hear the engine come to life."

"I think we know how to turn a key," Sean said, sounding vaguely amused.

Dave ignored him. "Shifting gears is done with this lever on the left side," he continued, tapping the gear shift. "Squeeze the clutch while you move it up or down to change gears. When you're ready to stop, just ease off the gas and apply the brakes—front brake on the right handlebar, rear brake by your right foot."

Peyton nodded, studying the bike as she followed along.

"Stay on designated trails as much as possible," Dave added, his gaze serious. "Yellowstone may be beautiful, but it can be dangerous if you're not careful. And make sure to keep an eye out for any signs of Frank—you never know what he might have left behind."

As Peyton climbed onto her ATV, she felt a sudden awareness of her vulnerability. Out here, surrounded by nature's raw power, it was easy to see how someone could lose themselves.

She glanced over at Sean, who was already perched on his own vehicle. He gave her an encouraging nod.

"Ready?" he asked, his voice barely audible above the rumble of their engines.

"Ready," she said, swallowing her nerves and gripping the handlebars.

Just as they were about to head out, Dave stepped forward, raising a hand for them to pause. He looked into Peyton's eyes, his expression grave. "Before you go, I should warn you—Frank may have a thing for primitive tools, but he's also a gun nut. I don't know him that well..." He paused, looking troubled.

"What?" Sean asked. "Spit it out."

"But from what I do know of him," Dave continued, "he's of the 'shoot first, ask questions later' variety. So you'd better pray you see him before he sees you."

CHAPTER NINE

The roar of the ATV's engine cut through the dense forest as Peyton raced along the dirt path. A low-hanging branch loomed ahead, and she ducked just in time to avoid it, sending a cascade of leaves fluttering down around her.

"Sean!" she shouted over her shoulder. "Watch out for the branch!"

To her surprise, however, there was no sign of Sean behind her. Instead, only the winding trail stretched back into the shadows. Confused and worried, Peyton slammed on the brakes, skidding to a stop amid a cloud of dust.

"Where could he be?" she muttered under her breath, straining her ears for any sound of her companion. The area was thick with towering pines, and their needles formed a soft carpet beneath the trees. Dappled sunlight filtered through the canopy, casting an intricate pattern on the ground.

Peyton racked her brain, trying to recall when she had last seen Sean in the hour since they'd left the ranger lodge. Her mind flickered back to about ten minutes ago when they had stopped at a fork in the path, debating which way to go. She had chosen the left path, while Sean had hesitated for a moment before ultimately agreeing. And now he was gone.

"Did he get lost?" Peyton wondered. The wilderness was vast, and even someone as experienced as Sean could find themselves disoriented.

Peyton killed the engine of her ATV, allowing the silence of the forest to envelop her. The distant chatter of birds and the rustle of leaves overhead filled the air as she strained her ears for any sign of Sean. She heard nothing but the sounds of the wilderness, however, and her worry deepened.

"Where are you, Sean?" she whispered to herself, the words swallowed by the vast expanse of nature surrounding her.

With a sigh, she restarted the engine and steered her ATV back down the path she had just traveled. Her eyes darted from side to side, studying the trail for any indication of where Sean might have gone.

As she rounded a bend in the path, Peyton caught sight of a familiar figure and slammed on the brakes. Sean stood there, startled, his eyes wide with surprise. He jumped to the side just before the ATV would have slammed into him, his body crashing into the underbrush with a grunt.

"Sean!" Peyton said, relief flooding her voice. "Are you alright?"

Grimacing, he untangled himself from a thorny bush and staggered back onto the path. "Yeah, I'm fine," he replied, brushing dirt and leaves off his clothes. "My engine died."

He gestured toward his ATV, which sat some distance down the path. His lean face held a mixture of frustration and confusion. "It just gave out suddenly," he said, running a hand through his hair.

"Did you run out of gas?" Peyton asked as she eyed his abandoned ATV.

Sean's eyes flashed with impatience. "No, I already checked the gas tank. I have over half a tank left." He gestured toward Peyton's ATV. "We'll just have to ride together on yours. Make room for me."

Peyton couldn't help but bristle at his tone. She knew they were pressed for time, but she was tired of his bad attitude. Now was as good a time as any to clear the air.

"Why do you have such a problem with me?" she asked.

"Problem? I don't have a problem with you." He reached out for her ATV. Peyton, frustrated at his denial, hit the reverse pedal with the heel of her foot and shot back out of his reach.

"Stop being childish," he said, reaching for the handlebars this time. Once more, she maneuvered away from him, her dark hair whipping around her face as she did so.

"Seriously?" He stared at her, incredulity etched into his features. "You're not going to let me ride with you?"

"Answer my question first," Peyton said, her gaze locked onto his. "Why do you have a problem with me?"

A tense silence settled between them as they faced off, both of their ATVs idling noisily in the background. Peyton did feel childish doing this, but she reminded herself that all she wanted was to be treated with respect. Whatever his problem with her was, she wanted to address it as soon as possible so that they could start functioning like an actual team. She needed that personally, yes, but even more importantly, Elisabeth Hall's life might depend on it.

Sean turned away in disgust, muttering under his breath. "I can't believe this." He pulled out his phone and held it above his head, eyes scanning for any bars of signal.

Peyton watched him, frustration simmering beneath the surface. "You know, since the moment I met you, you've been cold and aloof," she said, her voice breaking the silence that had settled between them. "Why can't you treat me like a decent human being?"

"A decent human being would give me a ride," he shot back, still waving his phone futilely in the air.

Peyton bit back an angry retort. Instead, she said, "Look, we need to work together on this case. And there's no telling whether or not we'll have to work together again in the future. We might never be friends, but can't we at least be civil? Can't we at least show each other some respect?"

With a heavy sigh, Sean gave up on finding a signal and shoved his phone back into his pocket, clearly frustrated. Running his hands through his hair, he stared at her, anger and annoyance mingling in his eyes.

"My previous partner was killed, alright?" he said.

Peyton stared at him, surprised by this confession.

"Gabriela Esposito," he said, swallowing hard and looking away. "She was my partner for three years. We were tracking a serial arsonist. We'd finally cornered him in an abandoned warehouse, but we didn't know he'd rigged the whole place with explosives."

As Sean continued, the sunlight filtering through the dense canopy cast dappled shadows across his face, accentuating the pain etched into his features. "The blast...it was massive. I barely made it out alive. Gabriela didn't." His voice cracked, and he clenched his fists, knuckles white. "It took months to track down the bastard who did it. He's serving multiple life sentences now, but that doesn't bring her back."

The weight of his words settled heavily around them, and Peyton felt her breath catch in her chest. She couldn't begin to imagine the anguish that haunted him.

"Is that why you're so distant with me?" she asked in a softer voice. "Because you're afraid something will happen to me too?"

He shook his head, his voice bitter. "I don't care what happens to you because I hardly know you. And I want to keep it that way. I won't let myself get attached again. It's too damn risky."

His words stung, but Peyton understood. He was just trying to protect himself from further pain. His aloofness toward her wasn't personal in the slightest—he would have treated any other new partner the same way. Peyton felt her frustration dissolve in the face of his vulnerability.

"Now can we please get out of here?" Sean asked wearily.

Peyton nodded and drove slowly forward, coming to a stop beside him. He climbed onto the ATV, placing his hands around her waist. It was an oddly intimate posture, but it didn't bother her the way it would have before his confession about his partner. He seemed more human now, more real.

The ATV roared beneath her as she navigated the winding trail. She could feel Sean's presence behind her, his body tense against hers as they pressed forward into the heart of Yellowstone. In the aftermath of their conversation, she found herself pondering his words and actions, finally understanding the source of his coldness.

As the shock of his revelation about Gabriela slowly dissipated, a wave of sympathy washed over her. The burden of grief Sean carried was immense, and she couldn't help but feel for him. No longer angry, a newfound sense of camaraderie blossomed in her chest. She knew now that they were both haunted by loss, bound together by the ghosts of their pasts.

As she rounded a corner, the trees gave way to an expansive meadow, the golden grasses swaying gently in the afternoon breeze. A feeling of vulnerability settled over her as they entered the open space, leaving behind the shelter of the forest. She glanced back at Sean, whose eyes scanned the area with guarded vigilance.

"I just wanted you to know," she began, raising her voice to be heard above the engine, "that if you ever want to talk about Gabriela, I'm here for you. We're in this together."

Before he could respond, Sean's gaze snapped forward, his eyes widening in alarm. Peyton looked forward, too. A couple hundred yards away, a figure was standing on the brow of a low ridge, his feet planted wide and a rifle in his hands.

He was aiming right at them.

CHAPTER TEN

Time seemed to slow as Sean's strong arms encircled Peyton's waist, yanking her from the ATV with a force that stole her breath. They hit the ground together, her body colliding with the soft grass and vibrant wildflowers. The world spun around her, a blur of greens and blues.

A gunshot cracked through the air, making her pulse thud in her ears. As her disorientation faded, the reality of their situation sunk in. If Sean hadn't pulled her off the ATV, she might have been shot.

Still, she didn't like lying there helplessly in the grass. She needed to get eyes on Petrel. She started to rise, but Sean's hand clamped down on her shoulder, forcing her back into the concealing embrace of the grass.

"Stay down," he hissed, his eyes scanning the ridge. "The shooter can't see us from here. We need to stay concealed."

Peyton's fingers wrapped around the grip of her handgun, but she knew it was no match for the rifle pointed in their direction. "He could be getting away," she said. "We can't let that happen."

"Trust me, I know," Sean said. He looked torn, caught between wanting to protect Peyton and apprehending Petrel.

"We have to do something," she insisted, her mind already working through possible strategies. The man was within their grasp, and she couldn't let him slip away.

"You're right," he finally said, his voice low and resolute. "Whatever happens, stay down, okay?"

"Wait, what are you going to do?" she asked, her heart pounding in her chest, refusing to sit idly by while her partner faced danger alone.

A sly grin spread across Sean's face, and a spark of determination ignited in his eyes. "I'm going to make sure Petrel doesn't get away." With that, he rose from the grass and began trotting toward the ridge, his body low and movements fluid, like a predator stalking its prey.

"Damn it, Sean," Peyton muttered under her breath. She couldn't just lie there while he risked everything. Pushing herself up, she quickly surveyed the area, trying to locate the shooter. The gunman remained hidden, but her eyes caught sight of an old cabin nearby. It stood weathered and sagging, its wooden walls peppered with signs of decay. The once-vibrant red paint had faded to a dull, rusty hue, and the roof was missing several shingles.

In the opposite direction, the ATV they had been riding lay partially concealed within some bushes, its wheels still spinning slowly.

A sudden, deafening crack of gunfire tore through the air, and Peyton's heart clenched in her chest. She watched, wide-eyed, as an ATV burst into view from behind the cabin, tires kicking up dirt and debris. It was Petrel, his face a twisted mask of determination, his rifle bouncing in his lap as he squeezed off another shot in their general direction. It was impossible for him to aim the rifle with one hand, but perhaps he was hoping to scare them into staying where they were.

"Sean!" Peyton shouted, her voice barely audible over the roar of the engine. He had already spotted Petrel, though, and was sprinting toward the ATV that had crashed into the bushes. Without a moment's hesitation, Peyton followed suit.

"Wait!" she cried out, her voice strained as she raced to catch up with Sean. He didn't seem to hear her, or else he simply chose to ignore her plea. As he reached the ATV and revved the engine, Peyton lunged forward, managing to grip onto the back of the vehicle just as it jolted into motion.

Noticing her, Sean clenched his jaw. For a moment it looked like he would keep on speeding ahead, letting the ATV drag her, but then he slowed.

Panting, Peyton climbed behind Sean. No sooner had she done so than the ATV shot forward again. The wind whipped at her face, stinging her eyes and tugging at her dark hair as they sped after Petrel.

She clung tightly to the sides of the ATV, her knuckles white with the effort. In that moment, she realized what was driving Sean—the memory of his lost partner, Gabriela. He'd do anything to prevent history from repeating itself, even if it meant risking his own life.

The wind whipped through Peyton's hair as the ATV roared beneath her, the powerful engine driving them relentlessly along the rugged trail. Sean's skilled driving narrowed the gap between them and their quarry with every passing second. As they rounded a sharp bend, Peyton caught sight of Petrel's ATV up ahead, weaving through the forest at breakneck speed, his figure barely visible through the trees.

"Look!" she shouted, pointing toward him. "We're gaining on him!"

Petrel glanced anxiously over his shoulder, his eyes widening in alarm as he realized that his pursuers had narrowed the distance. He gunned the engine, attempting to put more distance between them, but it was clear that he wouldn't be able to outrun them for long.

Suddenly, Peyton noticed a strange liquid running down the side of their ATV, glistening in the dappled sunlight filtering through the trees above. She tapped Sean's shoulder and pointed it out to him.

"Shit," Sean muttered under his breath, assessing the situation in an instant. "A bullet must have punctured the fuel tank. We don't have much time before we're out of gas."

"Get close to Petrel's ATV," Peyton said as a plan suddenly formed in her mind. "I'll jump across."

"Are you crazy? You'll get yourself killed!"

"We don't have time to argue!" she insisted, her heart pounding in her chest. "It's our only chance. We need to stop him before he gets away, and this is the best shot we've got."

Sean shook his head. "I can't let you do that," he said firmly. "It's too risky. We'll find another way to stop him."

"There *is* no other way. You're just gonna have to trust me."

"And what happens when you get yourself killed? I don't want your death on my conscience."

"And what about Elisabeth Hall's?" she asked, her frustration mounting. "Do you want her death on your conscience?"

Sean hesitated for a moment, his jaw clenched as he weighed the risks. Finally, he nodded. "Okay. I'll get us as close as I can. But you have to be quick."

Sean maneuvered their ATV closer to Petrel's. Peyton braced herself for the jump, her muscles tensing as she prepared to launch herself across the gap between the two vehicles. The wind whipped at her face, stinging her eyes and tangling her dark hair.

"Get ready!" Sean shouted over the noise, his eyes locked on their target.

But just as they rounded a bend, a massive boulder loomed ahead, jutting out from the landscape like a sentinel. With only a split second to react, Sean swerved hard, narrowly avoiding a collision that would have left them both injured—or worse. The sudden movement threw Peyton off balance, her grip tightening on Sean's waist as she fought to stay upright.

"Damn it!" she said under her breath, her heart hammering in her chest.

Once they had put the boulder behind them, Sean accelerated again, drawing them ever closer to Petrel's ATV. This time, however, he kept his gaze fixed on the terrain ahead, scanning for any further obstacles. As the gap between the two ATVs narrowed, Peyton took a deep breath, steeling herself for the leap.

"Go, now!" Sean yelled, and without hesitation, Peyton pushed off with every ounce of strength she could muster, launching herself through the air toward Petrel's speeding vehicle.

For a terrifying moment, she felt weightless, suspended above the ground with nothing but empty space beneath her. Her fingers grasped desperately at the rear of Petrel's ATV, and she barely managed to hold on as her legs slammed against the side of the vehicle. The impact sent a jolt of pain rocketing through her body, but she gritted her teeth and ignored it.

"Stop!" Peyton shouted. But Petrel only responded with a vicious swing of his elbow, aimed directly at her face. She ducked just in time.

"Enough!" she yelled, wrapping one arm around his neck and pulling him into a tight headlock. He struggled against her, clawing at her arm, but she refused to let go. With a choking gasp, Petrel finally relented, taking his foot off the gas and allowing the ATV to slow down.

"Please," he wheezed, his face turning red from the pressure of her grip. "Let go..."

The ATV's engine whined as it slowed to a crawl. With one final shove, Peyton pushed Petrel off the vehicle, his body thudding against the earth. He hit the ground hard, gasping and rubbing at his bruised throat. She jumped down from the ATV with practiced agility, immediately drawing her weapon and aiming it at him.

"Stay down!" she warned.

From the corner of her eye, she caught sight of Sean, who had been forced to abandon his own ATV after it ran out of gas. He jogged toward them, sweat glistening on his furrowed brow, his eyes wide with concern.

"Peyton!" he said, his breathing heavy. "Are you okay?"

Peyton met his gaze, searching for any sign of doubt or fear in those striking blue eyes. Instead, she saw only respect—and perhaps a trace of admiration. She allowed herself a small, triumphant smile, feeling a surge of pride well up inside her.

"I told you I could handle myself," she said.

Just then, a light rain began to fall. Peyton looked up, letting the cold water strike her upturned face.

"Long way back to the nearest ranger station," Sean said, looking thoughtful. "We'll be soaked by the time we get there."

"You have a better idea?"

He nodded, gazing back the way they'd come. "Yeah, I think I do."

CHAPTER ELEVEN

"Are you sure this is a good idea?" Peyton asked Sean in a low voice as they approached Frank Petrel's cabin.

The rain was falling in heavy drops, drenching the trio and making the earth beneath their feet slippery and treacherous. Petrel, his hands cuffed behind him, trudged a few steps ahead, his face a mask of barely contained anger.

Fortunately, they had both ATVs at their disposal for whenever they decided to leave. After they'd handcuffed Petrel, Sean had managed to patch the hole in their ATV's gas tank using a roll of duct tape he'd found in a basket attached to the ATV. Then, he siphoned some gas from Petrel's ATV so they could drive both vehicles back. Sean had ridden with Petrel, keeping a close watch on him as they navigated the rocky terrain.

Now, as they approached the cabin, Peyton could see Sean considering her words. It would be dangerous to let Petrel enter the cabin ahead of him, since there was no telling what might be inside.

As Petrel neared the cabin door, Sean shouted at him to stop. The disgraced park ranger froze in place, his sullen expression matching the stormy sky above as he turned back to look at them.

"Can't have you going in there and pulling out a weapon from some hiding place," Sean said. He opened the door and stepped inside the cabin to search it before allowing anyone else in.

Peyton watched the door close behind Sean, feeling the cold rain seeping through her clothes. She felt uneasy, remembering the stories of Petrel's harassment toward female tourists. The sooner they got this interview over, the better.

As the sound of rummaging came from within, Peyton sensed Petrel's gaze crawling over her like a swarm of insects.

"Never seen you before," Petrel said, his voice slimy and insinuating. "How long you been with the NPS, sweetheart?"

Peyton's jaw tightened, but she gave him no response. She wasn't about to do him the satisfaction of engaging him in conversation.

The cabin door creaked open again, revealing Sean carrying an assortment of weapons—a hunting knife with a serrated edge, a rusted machete, and a revolver that had seen better days. He tossed them aside in a wet thud, then gestured for them to enter. "We can talk inside now," he said.

With a nod, Peyton followed Petrel into the dim cabin, her senses on high alert. The room smelled of damp wood and stale cigarette smoke. A single oil lamp cast flickering shadows across the walls, which were adorned with a mishmash of animal skulls and worn maps. A small potbelly stove stood in one corner, while a simple cot took up the opposite space.

"Built this place myself," Petrel said, puffing out his chest as if the cabin were some grand achievement. "Took me three summers, working my fingers to the bone. Yep, I felled and stripped every one of these logs. Takes a lot of know-how to notch them and fit them together—ain't like building with Lincoln logs. Then you gotta chink the gaps with moss, and..."

Peyton stopped listening. Her eyes were roving around the room, searching for anything that might connect Petrel to Elisabeth Hall's disappearance. Near the stove, she spotted a dirty ashtray overflowing with cigarette butts—the same brand as those found near Elisabeth's RV.

"You smoke a lot?" she asked coolly, cutting through Petrel's rambling monologue. She gestured toward the ashtray, her eyes never leaving his face.

He shrugged, looking a bit offended at her interruption. "On occasion. Why, is that a crime?"

"No," Sean said. "But what is a crime is returning to park property while you're on disciplinary leave. You're not supposed to be here, Mr. Petrel."

Petrel let out a heavy sigh, his shoulders slumping. "I know it's against protocol for me to be on park property while suspended," he said, the remorse in his voice sounding forced to Peyton. "But I just love the wilderness so much. I didn't want to leave. Besides, I'm not harming anyone here, so what does it matter?"

"Maybe not," Sean said mildly. "But the harassment charges that got you put on disciplinary leave in the first place? You could argue those did some harm."

"Blown out of proportion," Petrel scoffed, shaking his head in disgust. "My interactions with those women were consensual. They led me on, and then they turned on me."

Listening to Petrel's pathetic excuses, Peyton couldn't help but feel a surge of revulsion. He was definitely a creep, that much was clear. But was he a murderer? As she continued to scan the cabin, she searched for any signs that he might have kidnapped women and brought them here. Yet, nothing seemed to stand out.

"Those are nice boots," Sean said suddenly. "Look very comfortable."

"These?" Petrel raised one of his feet in the air, examining the boot. "Nah, not all that great. These are just what I was issued for working in the park."

Sean nodded. Peyton could tell from the look in his eye, however, that he'd learned what he needed to learn.

"You know," Sean began slowly, "that's the same type of boot print that was found outside the RV of Elisabeth Hall—the woman who just went missing yesterday. Someone was smoking the same type of cigarettes, too. Funny coincidence, isn't it?"

A flicker of panic crossed Petrel's face before he composed himself. "Okay, fine. I was there, but only because I wanted to get a look at her. I didn't do anything, I swear."

Peyton studied his face carefully, trying to determine if he was telling the truth. Her gut told her that this man was dangerous, but she needed to be certain. She needed to push him further.

"How long did you watch her?" she asked.

Petrel hesitated, shifting uncomfortably under their scrutiny. "I don't know," he said, his gaze darting between them. "An hour, maybe? But I didn't touch her or hurt her."

"What got you interested in her in the first place?" Peyton asked.

Petrel shrugged. "Bumped into her on the trail. Good-looking gal." His cheek twitched, and Peyton sensed there was more.

"Did you try to make a move on her?" she asked.

Petrel shook his head in disgust. "All I was doing was keeping her from falling—she slipped in a patch of mud, and I reached out to steady her. Honest. Next thing I know, she's calling me a creep and warning me to stay back." His jaw clenched.

"Must've made you pretty angry," Sean said. "Hearing that on top of what those other women said about you."

Petrel hesitated, his eyes darting back and forth between Sean and Peyton, before admitting, "Yeah, it made me angry. Damn right it did." He clenched his fists, the handcuffs around his wrists clinking.

"Is that why you went to her RV?" Sean asked, keeping his tone conversational. "To get revenge?"

"Look, I'm not stupid," Petrel replied, growing wary. "I knew better than to do something like that."

"Really?" Sean asked, sounding almost disappointed. "Because if it were me, I'd want her – and all those other women – to know they couldn't just treat me like crap and get away with it."

Peyton observed the emotions playing across Petrel's face: anger, indignation, and finally a bitter rage that he could no longer contain. "You know what? Yeah, I wanted to hurt them. They humiliated me, went behind my back, and talked to my supervisor like I was some kind of predator! And he just took their word for it, without even giving me a chance!"

Sean shook his head sympathetically. "Didn't even let you tell your side of the story, did he?"

"Not for a second! He was quick to believe all those women just because they banded together like some sort of mob!" Petrel spat out the words with venom.

Peyton watched as Petrel's hands clenched and unclenched, the veins in his neck bulging. She knew that they were treading on dangerous ground, but she had to know. "What about Elisabeth?" she asked softly. "Did you want to hurt her, too?"

Petrel's expression turned stony. "I already said I didn't touch her."

"Come on," Sean said, with a tone that suggested they were old pals. "You must have thought about it."

Petrel shrugged defensively. "Sure, it crossed my mind."

"Did you fantasize about it?"

Petrel hesitated. "A little."

"And what did you fantasize about?"

"Choking her," Petrel admitted, his voice barely more than a whisper. He avoided their eyes, his face reddening with shame and anger.

Peyton's stomach clenched, and she wondered if they were finally getting closer to the truth. Was this deranged man responsible for Elisabeth's disappearance?

"Exactly when did you visit her RV, Frank?" Sean asked.

"Yesterday afternoon," he replied, his voice tense.

That fit with the timeline of Elisabeth's disappearance—she'd gone missing sometime yesterday evening. Peyton's heart raced as she considered the implications of Petrel's admission. She needed to establish whether he had an alibi for the time Elisabeth vanished.

"What did you do after that?" she asked.

"Left the park," Petrel said defensively. "Went into town, got some food, and hung out at a bar."

"Which bar?" Peyton asked, hoping to find a crack in his story.

"Rusty's Tavern," he replied, his tone defiant. "I was there most of the evening and night."

"Did anyone see you there? Anyone you talked to or interacted with?"

"Sure, the bartender knows me, and I talked to a few people. Played some pool." Petrel crossed his arms, appearing more confident now that he had provided a seemingly solid alibi.

Peyton's heart sank as she glanced at Sean, who seemed to share her disappointment. It appeared that Frank Petrel, despite his obvious anger and violent fantasies, couldn't have been the one who kidnapped Elisabeth. They would have to double-check the alibi, but if it held up, then they would be out of leads.

"Can you take off the cuffs now?" Petrel asked, his voice tinged with desperation.

"Hell no," Sean said, dropping the chummy act. "You shot at two federal employees. You're not getting off the hook that easily." He grabbed Petrel by the arm and pulled him out of the cabin into the downpour. Peyton followed, troubled.

The rain soaked through their clothes as they made their way to the ATVs. Droplets clung to Sean's lashes as he secured Petrel onto one of the vehicles. With a final tug on the restraints, he walked over to join Peyton, concern etched across his angular face.

"What are you thinking?" he asked.

"I'm disappointed," she said. "He was a very promising suspect. We'll still have to look into his alibi, but it sounds legitimate."

Sean nodded, his eyes darkening with frustration. "It looks like we're back to square one."

"Sort of," Peyton said. "The only difference is that now Elisabeth Hall has even less time to live. If the killer keeps to his pattern, then we have less than twenty-four hours to find Elisabeth—and the clock is ticking."

CHAPTER TWELVE

Charon raced through the damp, verdant woods, his heart pounding with exhilaration. A light rain drizzled from the sky, casting a shimmering veil over the dense foliage. The scent of damp earth and wet pine needles filled his nostrils, invigorating him.

This was his domain—the hunt, the pursuit. As he scanned the forest around him, he couldn't help but feel alive in a way that only the prospect of a sacrifice could rival.

His keen ears picked up the distant rustling of leaves and the occasional snap of a twig as he slowed to listen. The area was wild and untamed, a tangle of towering pines and thick underbrush that made it difficult for anyone to navigate. But not him. He had become one with these woods, a predator stalking its prey.

It had been a few hours since Elisabeth Hall had managed to slip away from him. She was more clever and determined than Charon had given her credit for. Every time he thought he had her cornered, she found a way to elude him.

But now, Charon believed he was finally closing in on her. There was a shape up ahead, huddled in the undergrowth. It had to be Elisabeth.

She must think I've lost her trail, Charon thought, amused.

He crept forward, every muscle tensed with anticipation. She must be exhausted by now. The thought of her fear, her desperation, only fueled his desire to capture her once more.

As he drew closer, however, the shape shifted, revealing itself to be a mule deer. Its eyes widened with fear, and it bolted away, disappearing into the foliage. A growl of frustration escaped Charon's lips.

"Damn it," he muttered under his breath, beginning to grow worried for the first time.

When she had first run off, he hadn't been worried—the vastness of Yellowstone and the isolation of this part of the park made it nearly impossible for her to find help. But as the afternoon wore on and darkness loomed, doubt began to creep in. Would she survive out here on her own? And if she did, how would he ever find her again in the dark?

Just then, his ears picked up the sound of approaching engines, their combined hum growing louder with each passing second. He tensed, crouching in the shadows, his eyes scanning through the trees for any sign of movement.

There was a flash of movement as a pair of ATVs raced by along a forest trail. Within moments, a desperate scream cut through the drone of the engines.

"Stop! Please, stop!" Elisabeth was shouting. Charon could see her silhouette as she raced after the ATVs, arms flailing. Despite her best efforts, however, the drivers didn't seem to have noticed her. The vehicles roared away into the distance, oblivious to her plight.

A sinister grin spread across Charon's face. At last, he had found her. His prey was within reach once more. Satisfaction coursed through his veins like a jolt of electricity.

"Where do you think you're going?" he called out, stepping from the shadows as he closed the distance between them. Elisabeth's gaze met his, terror etched on her face. She tried to sprint away, but fatigue weighed heavy on her limbs, and he caught up with her in a few bounding steps.

"Help!" she screamed, desperately trying to fight him off as he grabbed her. "Somebody, help me!"

"You just had a one-in-a-million shot at getting away," he said, his voice dripping with mockery. "And you blew it. You can fight all you want, but I promise you won't get another chance like that."

"Monster," she said, defiance burning in her eyes even as exhaustion threatened to overwhelm her. "Leave me alone. I'm not going back to that cage!"

With a nonchalant shrug, Charon hoisted Elisabeth up and threw her over his shoulder. Her fists pounded against his back, her protests reverberating through the damp forest. He ignored them, focusing instead on retracing his steps through the underbrush, whistling a jaunty tune as he went.

As they ventured deeper into the woods, Elisabeth's defiance gradually gave way to defeat, and her pounding grew weaker until it stopped altogether. Charon smirked, pleased with himself.

"Have to say, I'm impressed," he remarked, his voice a low rumble. "You evaded me longer than anyone ever has. You're even more worthy of being offered to the earth than I initially thought."

Silence hung between them for a moment, broken only by the sound of his footsteps and the patter of raindrops hitting leaves. Then Elisabeth spoke up, her voice weak but insistent.

"What went wrong for you, Charon?" she asked.

He furrowed his brow, genuinely puzzled. "What do you mean?"

"How did you become this...monster?"

A memory flickered in Charon's mind: a sickly-looking sheep lying in the mud, its breathing labored. His father handing him a knife, eyes hard and unyielding. The weight of expectation pressing down on him.

But just as quickly, he dismissed the recollection, unwilling to dwell on his past. Instead, he fixed his gaze on the trail ahead and responded coldly, "Nothing went wrong. I am who I am, just as you are who you are. Don't waste your time asking why; it won't change anything. The sooner you accept your fate, the happier you'll be."

Elisabeth remained quiet, her ragged breaths punctuating the air as Charon continued to carry her through the forest. Raindrops clung to his eyelashes, blurring his vision as the shadows grew longer and darkness crept closer. Despite the damp chill of the forest air, he couldn't help but feel a sense of satisfaction at having caught his quarry.

"Someone must have hurt you very badly," Elisabeth said suddenly. "Now you want to hurt others because you think it'll make you feel better. But it won't."

"Stop talking," Charon warned, annoyed.

Undeterred, she continued, "Hurting other people will never heal your wounds. Who hurt you? You should talk about it."

His anger surged, and without thinking, Charon threw Elisabeth to the mossy ground, her body crumpling like a ragdoll. She gasped, eyes wide with fear as he towered over her, his finger pointed accusingly in her face.

"You don't know a damn thing about me or what I've been through!" he snarled. "It's not time to sacrifice you just yet, but if you keep provoking me, I'll have no choice but to hurry things along!"

He looked away, his chest heaving with fury. The raindrops seemed to fall heavier now, mingling with the sweat on his brow. He closed his eyes, forcing himself to take slow, deep breaths. He shouldn't have let her get under his skin; he needed to be in control of his own emotions.

Elisabeth lay there, trembling and silent, her gaze never leaving his face. She seemed to understand that she had pushed him too far and that she might not survive long if she did so again.

"Get up," he finally said, his voice low and controlled. "We're going back, and this time you can carry yourself."

Elisabeth stared blankly at him for a few seconds, and he thought she might protest. Instead, she pushed herself shakily to her feet and began walking.

Charon stared at Elisabeth's back as she trudged forward, her footsteps small and hesitant. He had regained control over his emotions, but the forest seemed to close in on him, amplifying every sound and shadow. The rain continued to fall, soft droplets tapping against leaves and soaking into the damp earth.

"If you try running again," he warned, his voice low and dangerous, "I'll break one of your legs."

Elisabeth flinched at his words, but she didn't look back. She merely nodded and continued walking.

As they moved through the dense underbrush, Charon observed the way Elisabeth's eyes darted between tree trunks and scanned the forest floor, as if searching for any opportunity to escape. Her determination to live was almost admirable, even if it was futile.

"When are you planning to sacrifice me?" she asked. Her voice was soft, but even so, there was a firmness to it that told Charon he hadn't broken her yet—not entirely, anyway.

"Tomorrow," he replied, his tone matter-of-fact. He watched as Elisabeth's shoulders slumped further, and he felt a strange sense of satisfaction—not only in having the upper hand, but in knowing that he could still evoke fear, despite her earlier defiance.

"Before I do that, though," he continued, "I need to find the next one."

"Next what?" Elisabeth asked.

"The next sacrifice, of course," Charon said. "You didn't really think you were the last one, did you?" He chuckled. "No, my dear, this doesn't end with you."

"When does it end, then?" she asked in a faint voice.

He smiled. "When the earth is sated—which may take quite a while, because the earth is very, very hungry."

CHAPTER THIRTEEN

Raindrops splattered against the windshield of the sheriff's vehicle as it pulled away, carrying Frank Petrel into an uncertain future. Peyton, standing at the door of the small ranger's station where Dave Turner worked, watched curiously as the car disappeared down the winding road.

"I'm sure glad I'm not in his shoes," she said.

Sean, standing beside her, grunted in agreement. "It's not gonna be pretty," he said. "He'll likely face federal charges, and if he's convicted, I wouldn't be surprised if he gets a lengthy prison sentence."

Peyton nodded, her dark hair damp from the misty rain. While waiting for the sheriff to arrive earlier, she had investigated Petrel's alibi. He claimed to have been at Rusty's Tavern most of the night, and multiple people corroborated his story. He was a creep, certainly, and he would have to face the consequences of both shooting at a pair of federal agents and living on park property while on disciplinary leave, but nobody would be charging him with Elisabeth Hall's kidnapping any time soon.

With a sigh, Peyton turned her attention to the small ranger station, taking in the details of the room: the worn wooden floorboards that creaked beneath her boots, the dusty bookshelves lined with field guides and maps, and the scent of pine lingering in the air. In one corner, Dave sat in a rickety chair, flipping through a tattered wildlife magazine, his reading glasses perched on the tip of his nose. The neck brace he wore seemed to make every movement uncomfortable, but his stoicism never wavered.

"Anything interesting in there?" she asked, trying to be polite.

Dave glanced up, the warm lamplight casting shadows across his face. "Oh, you know, just brushing up on my bison facts," he replied, a hint of humor in his voice. "Did you know that a bison's hump is actually muscle? Helps them plow through the snow."

"Really?" Sean said, feigning surprise. "I thought it was just for show. Some people like big butts."

Peyton rolled her eyes at him. So he *did* have a sense of humor. A juvenile one, perhaps, but a sense of humor nonetheless.

"You got any coffee around here?" Sean asked, glancing inside a mug sitting on the edge of the desk.

"Sorry, man," Dave replied, not looking up from his reading. "Ran out this morning. All I've got is some old instant hot chocolate mix. A little stale, but still palatable. Want some?"

"As delicious as that sounds, I'm going to have to pass."

Dave shrugged. "Your loss."

As the cabin fell silent, Peyton's mind went back to what had happened back on the ATVs, while chasing after Petrel. She thought of Sean's protectiveness, his unwillingness to let her put herself in harm's way. She moved a short distance away from Dave and gestured for Sean to join her. He approached, frowning.

"About what happened earlier," Peyton said in a low voice, hoping Dave couldn't hear her. "I appreciate you wanting to protect me, but we need to face things together. We're partners, and that means we have to accept the risks equally."

Sean glanced away, his eyes narrowed as he stared out the window. The silence stretched between them, heavy with the weight of unspoken fears.

"I'm not going to lose another partner," he said quietly. "I wouldn't be able to live with myself."

She cracked a smile. "Believe it or not, I'm not planning to die any time soon."

Sean said nothing. He went on gazing blankly out the window.

"You're not responsible for Gabriela's death, you know," Peyton said. She sensed she needed to get through to Sean, needed him to recognize that he couldn't keep throwing himself in harm's way out of a misguided sense of penance.

"Whatever you're going through," she went on, "whatever demons you're fighting…don't hamstring this investigation by keeping me at arm's length, okay?"

A few beats passed in silence. Then Sean nodded, gazing at her somberly. "I hear you, Peyton." He sighed, rubbing his face. "Now can we wrap up this therapy session and focus on the case, please?"

Peyton gave him a wry smile. "You still haven't answered my question."

"What question?"

"About music. I said I liked folk music, and you said you didn't. But you didn't tell me what you *do* like."

Sean arched an eyebrow. "Really? It's that important to you?"

She continued to smile back at him, not backing down.

"Jazz," he said. "I like jazz. Happy?"

"What do you like about jazz?"

He took a deep breath and let it out slowly. "It's smooth. Unhurried. Helps me relax. Satisfied? Can we do our jobs now, or do you want to know my Zodiac, too?"

She tossed her shoulders, pleased with herself. "Just wanted to reciprocate."

He shook his head at her. "You're insufferable."

Peyton smiled again. Maybe, just maybe, there was still a chance they could eventually tolerate one another. For now, that was a lofty enough goal to aim for.

Peyton grabbed the back of a chair and leaned on it, growing serious as she considered where things stood with the investigation. "We need to figure out what all three victims have in common," she said.

"Well," Sean said, "they were all hiking in Yellowstone, and they were all women in their twenties or thirties. But beyond that..." He shook his head. "Ernestine Johnson was a photographer, Leticia Darrow was a waitress, and Elisabeth Hall was – *is* – a college student. Different backgrounds and lifestyles."

"Right," Peyton mused, rubbing her temples. "But there has to be *something* connecting them." She stared out the window, watching the rain streak down the glass panes, knowing that each moment they spent searching for answers could mean life or death for Elisabeth Hall.

A new idea occurred to her, and she turned around to face Sean. "By the way, did you ever hear back from the senator about his daughter's possible health condition?" she asked, remembering the immunosuppressants they had found in Elisabeth's RV.

"No, I never did," he answered, concern etched on his face. "Maybe it's time to give him another call."

"Good idea." Peyton picked up the old landline phone on the wall and dialed Senator Hall's number.

"Hello?" The voice that answered was not Senator Hall's; it was a little boy with a minor speech impediment, making his words sound slightly slurred and endearing. "Wh-who's this?"

"Hi there," Peyton said gently, taken aback by the unexpected response. "My name is Peyton Risk. I'm looking for Senator Joseph Hall. Is he available?"

"Joe? He's my uncle," the boy responded excitedly. "We're at his house for vacation!" The child's voice was filled with enthusiasm as he began to describe the various activities they had enjoyed during their visit. "Uncle Joe has a big pool, and I like to swim in it! And there's a cool game room with lots of toys and video games. His house is so different from mine—it's huge and fancy!"

It occurred to Peyton that Senator Hall must have gathered his extended family around him to provide support during this difficult time. It was a small, heartwarming detail amidst the chaos of the investigation.

Just then, she heard the senator's voice in the background, asking the boy who he was talking to. His tone was kind and gentle, a stark contrast to the stern demeanor he had displayed during their previous interactions.

"I'm telling the nice lady about why I like going on vacation, Uncle Joe," the boy replied innocently. The sound of the senator chuckling reached Peyton's ears, and she couldn't help but smile.

"Could you please give the phone to your uncle?" Peyton said gently, trying not to disrupt the tender moment between the senator and his nephew.

"Okay," the boy agreed, and she heard shuffling as the phone was handed over.

"Who is this?" the senator asked, his voice both friendly and guarded at the same time.

"Senator Hall," Peyton said. "It's Peyton Risk. We spoke earlier, at the morgue?"

Instantly, the senator's tone changed, growing cooler and more authoritative. "Ms. Risk, do you have an update on my daughter's case?"

"Well, I wanted you to know we found her RV, and we discovered something interesting in her medicine cabinet."

She waited, but the senator remained silent. After a few seconds, Peyton went on.

"Immunosuppressants," she said. "We found bottles of immunosuppressants. Is there a medical condition Elisabeth has that we should be aware of? It might be important to our investigation."

The rain pattered outside, its rhythm punctuating the tense silence that followed.

"Why are you focusing on this?" the senator asked. "You should be out there looking for the killer, not rummaging through my daughter's belongings!"

Peyton felt a surge of frustration but carefully kept her voice calm. "Senator, every detail matters in an investigation like this. If Elisabeth is sick, it could impact our search for her."

"Your priorities are misplaced, Ms. Risk," he said, his anger rising. "I'm starting to wonder if you're really the right person for the job, since you clearly don't understand what's important here."

Peyton clenched her jaw, refusing to let the senator's anger derail her focus. "Senator Hall, with all due respect, you are not a trained investigator. I am," she said firmly, gathering her resolve. Her mind briefly flickered back to the countless hours spent poring over evidence and building profiles during her five years in the FBI. She knew the criminal mind, understood its patterns and deceptions.

"If you want to find a way to get me taken off this case, that's your prerogative," she continued, her gaze fixed on the raindrops tracing paths down the windowpane. "But I assure you, I *am* the best person for this job. If you truly want Elisabeth found, then I need you to stop working against me and start cooperating."

A heavy silence lingered on the line, punctuated only by the faint sound of the senator's breathing. Peyton took a deep, calming breath herself, trying to center her thoughts. She needed answers, and antagonizing the senator wouldn't help.

The silence stretched on for a few more agonizing seconds before the senator finally spoke. "Elisabeth has a rare autoimmune disease called scleroderma. It affects her skin, blood vessels, and internal organs. The immunosuppressants help control the inflammation and slow down the progression."

As the senator described the disease, Peyton felt a pang of sympathy for Elisabeth, imagining the struggle she must have faced each day.

"She's a fighter, though," Senator Hall added, his voice cracking slightly. "The doctors didn't think she'd live as long as she has, but she keeps defying their expectations. That's why she was out in Yellowstone—she wanted a chance to be alone for a while, to clear her head and think about what she wanted to do with the time she has left."

The senator's words painted a vivid image of Elisabeth in Peyton's mind: a determined young woman, grappling with her own mortality, seeking solace in nature's embrace. It only strengthened her resolve to find her and bring her home safe.

"That was Judd's idea, actually," Hall added.

"Judd?" Peyton asked.

"Judd Masterson, her therapist. When she learned about the severity of her condition, she decided to start seeing a counselor. Needed someone to help her stay positive, you know—keep her mind in the right place."

"Thank you for telling me all this, senator," Peyton said softly, her voice filled with compassion. "Where was she going for treatment?"

"New Beginnings Wellness Clinic," he replied, his voice subdued.

Peyton could hear the weariness in his tone, and she tried to offer some comfort. "I understand how difficult this must be for you, but I assure you we'll do everything in our power to get Elisabeth safely back to you."

"Thank you," he said, a hint of an apology in his voice. "I just...I want my daughter back. That's all that matters now."

Peyton ended the call with a solemn nod, even though the senator couldn't see it. She turned to find Sean and Dave laughing about something, their camaraderie a stark contrast to the weight of the conversation she'd just had. Sean caught her eye, and his laughter faded into concern.

"Hey, what did the senator say?" he asked, his eyes searching hers.

"Elisabeth has a rare autoimmune disease called scleroderma," she explained. "The immunosuppressants were to control the inflammation and slow down the progression."

Sean's brow furrowed, his lips pressing into a thin line. "If that's the case, then what happens if she stops taking them?"

Peyton shook her head, dread settling in the pit of her stomach. "I'm not an expert, but from what I understand, it's not good."

"Not good? What does that mean?"

Peyton hesitated, then swallowed hard. "If she goes too long without medication...her organs could fail."

CHAPTER FOURTEEN

Peyton stared out the window of the car, her eyes locked with the unfriendly-looking dog. Its dark, mottled fur bristled, and a low growl rumbled from its throat.

Nothing like laying out the red carpet, she thought wryly.

The dog was a muscular mix of Rottweiler and pitbull, standing like a sentry between them and their destination: the house of Gus Darrow, widower to Leticia Darrow. The dog's bared teeth and tense posture screamed readiness to attack as soon as Peyton dared to step out.

"Got any bright ideas?" she asked Sean, who was sitting in the passenger seat, his eyebrows raised.

"Maybe we should go to the store and buy a T-bone steak," he said.

"Ha-ha," Peyton said dryly.

The Darrows' residence was on the outskirts of a town not far from Yellowstone. The area looked weather-beaten and neglected, with patches of overgrown grass and wildflowers peeking through the cracks in the sidewalk. The house itself had once been white but had faded to a dull gray over time. It stood solitary among the other modest homes, each separated by wide stretches of land. A chain-link fence enclosed the backyard, a creaky gate hanging slightly ajar.

Taking a deep breath, Peyton decided to try a new approach. She carefully lowered her window just a few inches and attempted to speak to the dog in the calmest voice she could muster. "Hey there," she said. "It's alright, we're not here to hurt anyone."

Instead of calming down, however, the dog seemed to grow angrier at the sound of Peyton's voice. With a guttural snarl, it lunged at the window, snapping its teeth viciously.

"Okay, that was a bad idea," Peyton said, quickly rolling up the window as the dog continued to snarl outside.

Just then, the front door of the house swung open, and a man stepped out onto the porch. He was squat and thick, with unkempt brown hair and deep-set eyes that were shadowed by grief. The man shouted something unintelligible at the dog, who hesitated as if unsure whether or not to obey.

"Chopper, heel!" the man shouted again, this time more forcefully. To Peyton's surprise and relief, the dog obeyed, slinking away from the car to stand obediently at the man's side.

"Sorry about that," the man called over, his voice strained but apologetic, as he led the dog into the backyard and closed the gate behind it. Moments later, he returned, walking toward Peyton's and Sean's car with a somber expression.

Peyton and Sean exchanged a glance before cautiously stepping out of the vehicle. The man approached them, offering a weary smile. "I'm Gus Darrow," he said, extending a hand first to Peyton and then to Sean.

"Peyton Risk," she replied, shaking his hand firmly, feeling the rough texture of his calloused fingers. "This is my partner, Sean O'Malley."

"Nice to meet you both," Gus said, eying their NPS uniforms. "I suppose you're here about Leticia."

"Unfortunately, yes," Peyton replied softly. "We just want to ask you some questions about her to try to get a better understanding of who she was."

Gus nodded solemnly and waved for them to follow him.

Peyton followed Gus into his home, with Sean close behind. Peyton's first impression was that the house itself seemed to be weighed down by Gus's grief. The living room was disheveled and neglected. Unwashed dishes were piled high in the kitchen sink, their surfaces coated in dried food particles, while garbage spilled over from the brimming trash can.

Empty beer bottles adorned various surfaces, creating an atmosphere of despondency and despair. It was clear that Gus was struggling with the loss of his wife, leaving him overwhelmed by the simplest of daily tasks. Peyton felt a pang of sympathy for him.

"Have there been any developments in the case?" Gus asked.

"It's still very early in the investigation," Sean said. "But we'll let you know as soon as we know something."

Gus nodded, his gaze distant, as if he expected nothing less than uncertainty.

Peyton and Sean took their seats on a worn couch opposite Gus, trying to ignore the dog hairs that clung to their clothes. Gus gestured toward the coffee table, where a half-empty bottle of beer stood beside several glasses. "Can I offer you a drink?"

"Thank you, but we're fine," Peyton said, her eyes meeting Gus's, conveying a silent understanding of his loss.

"Alright then," Gus said, taking a deep breath. "What do you want to know?"

"How did you and Leticia meet?" Peyton asked, hoping to gain insight into the woman they were seeking to understand.

Gus's eyes softened as he began to recount their story. "It was at a local fair about eight years ago. I'd gone there with some friends, not expecting anything out of the ordinary. But then...there she was." A faint smile played on his lips, momentarily brightening his weary face. "She was working at one of the game booths, and her laughter was like...well, it was a melody. It drew me in like a moth to a flame."

Peyton nodded encouragingly.

"Her smile...it lit up the whole place," he continued, his voice thick with emotion. "I walked over to her booth, feigned interest in the game just to talk to her. When our eyes met, I felt this...connection, you know? Like we were meant to find each other."

Peyton could see how deeply Gus had loved Leticia—even now, as he spoke of their meeting, his face became animated, a stark contrast to the grief-stricken man they'd seen earlier.

"Anyway, I ended up winning that silly game and she awarded me the ugliest stuffed bear you've ever seen." Gus chuckled. "But I treasured that thing like it was made of gold because it represented the beginning of us."

It was a beautiful story, and Peyton couldn't help thinking that, as sad as it was that the Darrows had been separated after only eight years, many people never got to experience such love at all.

"Thank you for sharing," she said, resisting the urge to pull out her necklace and place it in her hand, just to feel its comforting weight as she thought about her own fractured family. "It sounds like you two were very happy."

Gus nodded, rubbing at the corner of his eye. "We were."

Sean cleared his throat and shifted his feet. "Did Leticia act strangely or out of character at all in the days leading up to her disappearance?" he asked.

Gus shook his head. "No, everything was completely normal—well, mostly. She did have a depressive episode about a month ago, but that's not uncommon for her."

Peyton studied him, curious. "Could you tell us more about these episodes? What usually triggers them?"

Gus sighed and rubbed his hands together, seemingly lost in thought. "She's been working too hard, putting too much on her own shoulders. Sometimes the weight just becomes too much for her to bear." He paused, his gaze distant and unfocused. If he was aware that he'd started speaking about his wife in the present tense, his face didn't show it.

"During those times," he continued, "she'd retreat into herself, barely speaking, hardly eating. It was like a dark cloud had settled over her, and I couldn't reach her no matter how hard I tried."

Peyton could feel Gus's pain as he described his wife's struggles, and it resonated with her own memories of loss. She made a mental note to explore Leticia's mental health further—it might hold a clue to her murder.

"Can you explain what you mean by 'working too hard'?" Sean asked, leaning forward slightly.

Gus looked at Sean, his expression grim. "Leticia was studying for her accounting degree while working part-time as a waitress. We had this plan, you see—" his voice cracked, but he continued, "—she'd get a high-paying accountant job, and we'd move somewhere better. Start fresh."

He glanced around the room, taking in the clutter and disarray that surrounded them. "This place isn't much, but we always dreamed of something better. A beautiful home, maybe somewhere near the mountains. A place where we could finally be happy and free of our past."

As Gus spoke, Peyton could see the dream home taking shape in her mind's eye: a quaint, cozy house nestled in a lush valley, sunlight streaming through the tall trees surrounding it. She could almost feel the warmth and love that would have filled such a place, and her heart ached for the future Gus and Leticia had been robbed of.

"Thank you for sharing all of this with us, Mr. Darrow," she said softly. "Every detail helps us get closer to understanding what happened to Leticia."

Gus nodded, his eyes filled with sorrow, but also determination. "I just want to know who did this to her…and why."

Peyton's gaze drifted toward the window, and she found herself thinking about Elisabeth Hall and the clinic she was receiving treatment at. Her intuition told her there must be more to Leticia's story than Gus had shared so far. She cleared her throat.

"Mr. Darrow," Peyton began, choosing her words carefully. "Did Leticia have any health conditions or diseases we should know about?"

Gus looked surprised by the question, his brow furrowing as he considered it. "No," he finally replied, shaking his head. "She didn't have any significant health issues. She was strong and healthy."

"Are you sure?" Sean asked, his eyes searching for any hint of uncertainty in Gus' face. "Sometimes people hide things, even from their loved ones."

"Of course, I'm sure," Gus said, a defensive edge creeping into his voice. "Leticia was my wife—I would've known if something was wrong."

Peyton could sense Gus' rising agitation, but she couldn't shake the feeling that there was some crucial piece of information missing from their conversation. She glanced over at Sean, who seemed equally stumped. They needed a new angle.

"Is there anyone who might have had a grudge against Leticia? Any enemies?" Sean asked.

Gus sighed heavily, rubbing his temples as if to ward off a headache. "I've been asked that same question over and over, and the answer is still no," he said, sounding discouraged. "Leticia was a very agreeable person; she kept to herself and never made any trouble with anyone."

The late afternoon sun cast long shadows across the room, making the clutter and disarray look even more chaotic. As Peyton observed Gus, she empathized with his pain but knew they couldn't afford to leave any stone unturned. In her mind, she retraced their conversation, searching for any overlooked details that might provide a clue to Leticia's fate.

"Is there anything else you can think of, no matter how small or insignificant it may seem?" she asked. "Sometimes the smallest detail can be the key to solving a case."

Gus stared at her for a moment, his eyes filled with a jumble of emotions—grief, frustration, and a desperate hope that they would find answers. Finally, he shook his head. "I've told you everything I know," he said quietly. "I just…I don't understand why this happened to her."

"Neither do we," Sean agreed somberly. "But rest assured, Mr. Darrow, we're going to do everything we can to find out."

He rose. A moment later, Peyton did the same, though she felt reluctant to leave. What hadn't she thought to ask? What was she missing?

"Thank you for your time, Mr. Darrow," Sean said, extending a hand. "We appreciate your help."

The two men shook hands. Then Peyton shook Gus's hand, though he avoided her eyes. He looked defeated, as if he had expected their visit to bring a sense of hope but he'd been sorely disappointed.

As Sean headed toward the door, Peyton paused and turned back to Gus. "One last question," she said softly. "Was Leticia seeing anyone about her depression? A professional, maybe?"

Gus's brow furrowed slightly, and he nodded. "Yeah, she was seeing a counselor. JM—that's what he went by."

Peyton glanced at Sean. JM? Then it clicked.

"Do you mean Judd Masterson?" she asked, surprised.

Gus nodded. "That's the fellow. Why? You heard of him before?"

"Yes," Peyton said softly, thinking of Senator Hall's words to them about Elisabeth and the therapist she was seeing. "Yes, we have."

CHAPTER FIFTEEN

Peyton knocked firmly on the heavy oak door. "Dr. Masterson? Judd Masterson, are you home?"

There was no answer. She peered in the window and found the interior dark and still, which seemed odd considering the half a dozen vehicles parked outside.

Judd Masterson's home doubled as his office, nestled within the breathtaking mountains near Yellowstone National Park. It was a luxurious dwelling, boasting an expansive wooden deck and floor-to-ceiling windows that showcased the surrounding natural beauty. The property sprawled across several acres of pristine wilderness, giving clients a sense of sanctuary and escape from the world outside.

Sean scanned the surroundings, an eyebrow raised in disbelief. "I didn't realize shrinks got paid so well," he mused. "Maybe I should become one."

Peyton ignored him, her sharp eyes scanning the area for any signs of life. Her ears perked up at the faint sound of soft music carried by the breeze. She noticed a dirt path winding into the woods, partially hidden by the shadows cast by tall pine trees. Fresh prints dented the soft earth, leading Peyton to believe someone had recently passed by. Without hesitation, she set off along the path, followed closely by Sean.

As they ventured deeper into the woods, the path grew narrower, the evergreen canopy above casting dappled light onto the forest floor. The music, a soothing melody played on a flute, grew louder with each step they took. As they rounded a bend in the path, the source of the music became apparent: a small clearing bathed in the warm glow of the setting sun, where a group of people sat cross-legged on the ground, eyes closed and faces serene.

A steep cliff rose dramatically behind the gathered group, adding an air of mystique to the scene. The strangest part, however, was the several llamas that roamed around the clearing. Some of the people reached out to pet the gentle creatures as they passed by, their expressions remaining calm and focused.

"Can't say this is what I was expecting," whispered Peyton. She glanced at Sean, who looked just as taken aback.

Peyton's gaze returned to the man leading the group. He was tall and lean with a mane of wavy gray hair that reached his shoulders. His chiseled features gave him an air of authority, which seemed to be amplified by the large snake draped around his shoulders. Its scales shimmered in shades of brown and green, a stark contrast against the man's white linen shirt. The sight of the large snake sent a ripple of unease down Peyton's spine.

"Focus on the rhythm of your breathing," the man said, his voice deep and soothing. "Allow the energy of the earth to rise through your feet, up your spine, and out through the crown of your head."

The group responded with slow, synchronized inhales and exhales, seemingly entranced by the man's guidance. Their faces relaxed, and their shoulders dropped as they surrendered themselves to the exercise.

"Looks like we found Dr. Masterson," murmured Peyton. What kind of therapy session had they stumbled upon? And how was it connected to the murdered women they were investigating?

Peyton and Sean carefully approached the group, their steps crunching on the forest floor. Just as they neared the edge of the clearing, Sean's foot came down on a pile of llama dung. "Ah, damn it," he muttered under his breath, trying to keep his voice low.

Dr. Masterson's head snapped in their direction, his eyes narrowing. He addressed the group without missing a beat, his voice still calm but with an edge of irritation. "Continue picturing your inner sanctuary and focus on your breathing."

Rising gracefully, Dr. Masterson strode toward Peyton and Sean. As he moved closer, the snake around his shoulders shifted lazily, its tongue flicking out to taste the air. Despite her unease, Peyton couldn't help but be fascinated by the creature. It was beautiful.

"Can I help you?" Dr. Masterson asked coolly, his gaze shifting between the two intruders.

"Are you Judd Masterson?" Sean asked, still trying to clean off his boot by dragging it along the ground.

"I am," he said. "What brings you here?"

"We'd like to speak with you about a few of your patients," Peyton said, meeting his gaze evenly.

"Seekers," Dr. Masterson corrected, a hint of a smile playing at the corners of his mouth. "I don't call them patients. They come to me seeking guidance, a path to a better life."

Peyton could see Sean's jaw clench, as if he were resisting the urge to roll his eyes. Instead, he crossed his arms over his chest and waited for the therapist to continue.

"Through my unique approach," Dr. Masterson said, his voice taking on a vague, New Age tone, "I help them connect with their inner selves, harnessing the energies of the earth and their own spiritual vibrations. These seekers learn to break free from the constraints of society and embrace their true potential."

A gentle nudge on Peyton's arm interrupted her thoughts, and she turned to see a curious llama standing beside her. Its soft, black eyes studied her, and its long, thick lashes fluttered. The animal had a cream-colored coat with patches of light brown, and its ears were perked up as if trying to listen intently.

"Ah, this is Socrates," Dr. Masterson said with a smile, his voice warm as he observed the interaction. "He likes to greet newcomers. Llamas are incredibly intuitive animals; they can sense a person's energy and emotions."

Peyton, unsure of how to respond, hesitantly reached out and patted the llama's neck. Socrates responded by nudging her again. It was actually rather endearing.

"Is there somewhere quieter we could speak?" Peyton asked, her gaze shifting back to Masterson.

"Unfortunately, I can't leave my seekers in the middle of a session," he replied, shaking his head. "They may need further guidance."

"How long will that take?" Sean asked, a hint of impatience in his voice.

"Could be a few more hours," Masterson said, keeping his voice low. "The importance of uninterrupted meditation cannot be overstated. It allows them to delve deeper into their subconscious, facilitating emotional healing and personal growth."

Sean shook his head firmly. "We can't wait that long. This is urgent."

As he took a step forward, the snake around Masterson's neck rose up, its head swaying slightly as it stared at Sean. The serpent flicked its tongue, tasting the air between them, and Sean took a wary step back.

"Abacus doesn't like aggressive energy," Masterson said, gently stroking the snake's glossy scales.

"Abacus?" Peyton asked, eyeing the creature.

"His name comes from the ancient calculating tool—a symbol of wisdom and knowledge. I received him as a gift from a shaman during my travels in South America."

"Regardless of your snake's preferences," Sean said, trying to maintain his composure, "we need to speak with you today."

"And I'm telling you that's just not possible," Masterson replied firmly, his eyes narrowing. "My seekers' needs come first. Unless you can provide me with a good reason for interrupting their session, I'm afraid our discussion will have to wait."

"How about murder?" Peyton asked.

Masterson froze. "What are you talking about?"

"I'm talking about two women who were seeing you, one of whom is now dead and the other is missing."

Masterson licked his lips, his eyes darting back to the group behind him. He looked trapped, unsure of himself. Then he regained his composure with a deep breath.

"Very well," he said. "But not here. I have a guesthouse nearby where we can speak privately."

As they followed Masterson past the meditating seekers, Peyton couldn't help but feel a sense of unease. Something about this situation felt off, but she couldn't quite put her finger on it. She glanced at Sean, who seemed equally tense, his jaw clenched as he kept his gaze focused straight ahead.

Masterson paused suddenly, pulling Abacus from around his neck. To Peyton's surprise, he thrust the snake at Sean, giving him no time to prepare.

"Why don't you leave Abacus over there by that pile of rocks?" he said, pointing. "He likes crawling in there."

Sean hesitated, looking momentarily uncertain. Then he took the large snake in his arms, his fingers steady despite the tension in his body. His eyes met Peyton's briefly, and she could see the determination in them. He wouldn't let Masterson intimidate him.

Masterson looked surprised. "You've handled snakes before," he said.

"A time or two," Sean said cryptically.

"Well, be careful with her. She's very delicate."

As Sean carried the snake to the pile of rocks, Peyton and Masterson continued walking toward the guesthouse, passing by a small pond where another group of seekers were gathered. Peyton watched as they dipped their feet in the water, their eyes closed as if in deep contemplation. She couldn't help but wonder what kind of techniques Masterson used to get his followers to such a state of focus.

Soon Peyton spotted the guesthouse, a large, rustic cabin surrounded by trees and shrubs. The white exterior gleamed in the waning light of early evening.

"Quite a setup you've got here," Peyton said, unable to hide her curiosity. "Is this for personal or professional use?"

"The latter," Masterson said, his eyes taking on a distant quality as though lost in thought. "I find that some of my seekers benefit from a more private, intimate environment. This guesthouse allows me to create the perfect space for them to confront their deepest fears and anxieties."

As they reached the guesthouse, Masterson swung open the door, gesturing for her to enter. An unsettling musky odor wafted out, and she hesitated for a moment before stepping inside.

The interior was dark, only faint slivers of light seeping through the closed blinds. It took a moment for her eyes to adjust, during which time she noticed a pair of glowing orbs staring back at her from the far end of the guesthouse.

Peyton felt as if a spider had just crawled across the nape of her neck.

"Exactly what kind of therapy do you use this place for?" she asked, turning around.

"Exposure therapy," he replied. He was now holding a small canister in his hand. He must have pulled it from his pocket. As Peyton stared at it, puzzled, he pressed the top of the canister, spraying her. She recoiled.

"What the hell?" she said, rubbing at her eyes, which were already beginning to burn. And what was that smell? Bacon?

"Just a little incentive for Marduk," Masterson said. "He likes it on his food." With that, he slammed the door shut. The sound cracked like a gunshot in the confined space, followed a moment later by the unmistakable click of a lock.

Panic surged through Peyton's veins as the reality of the situation sank in. "Dr. Masterson!" she cried, pounding on the door. "This isn't funny! Let me out!"

But there was no response, only the sound of her own desperate breathing—

And the low growl that emanated from the unseen creature in the darkness.

CHAPTER SIXTEEN

A deep, guttural growl rumbled through the darkness. Peyton swallowed hard, her hands trembling as she drew her weapon and aimed at the source of the sound.

"Please don't let it be what I think it is," she whispered under her breath, praying for some divine intervention to save her from this nightmare.

The creature – Marduk, Masterson had called it – approached, sniffing the air, its massive body gliding through the shadows. Its form briefly stepped into a sliver of light that filtered through a crack in the window, revealing the terrifying truth. The monstrous beast was a bear, larger than any she had ever seen before. Its thick, shaggy fur was a dark shade of brown, almost black, while its powerful muscles rippled beneath its coat. Piercing, intelligent eyes stared right at her, unyielding and hungry.

Peyton's breath caught in her throat as she realized she was trapped with this behemoth. She knew shooting it would only serve to anger the animal, and so, hesitantly, she lowered her weapon. Marduk advanced closer, still sniffing the air, drawn by the scent of bacon that clung to her like an unwanted second skin.

"Easy now," she muttered, trying to keep her voice steady and calm despite the panic welling up inside her. "You don't want me, big guy."

But Marduk seemed insistent. He stretched out his massive paw, gently touching her leg, leaving her acutely aware of the razor-sharp claws that could easily tear her apart. Peyton fought the urge to recoil, knowing that any sudden movement might trigger the bear's predatory instincts.

"Okay, buddy, just...stay calm," she said, more to herself than the bear, as she racked her brain for a way out of this deadly predicament.

The windows around her were small and narrow, offering no hope of escape. Then, at the far end of the guesthouse, she spotted a larger window—one that might just be big enough for her to fit through. But first, she had to find a way past Marduk.

"Think, Peyton, think," she whispered to herself. She needed something to distract the bear long enough for her to make a break for it.

Her eyes scanned the room, looking for anything that could serve as a diversion. And then, it occurred to her. Holstering her gun with trembling hands, she unzipped her windbreaker. It must have captured most of the bacon scent Masterson had sprayed at her.

Here goes nothing, she thought, holding out the jacket. Marduk smelled it, then reached out a paw.

Peyton pulled the jacket away and tossed it into the corner of the room. For a few seconds, Marduk just stared dumbly back at her, as if not understanding. Then he began to amble forward, sniffing the air and following the mouthwatering scent of the bacon.

This was her chance. Peyton moved quickly but quietly, keeping her eyes on the bear as she edged her way toward the window. Her heart was hammering in her chest, and she couldn't shake the fear that Marduk would turn back at any second.

Almost there, she thought, steeling her nerves as she slid along the wall, inching closer and closer to the window. She didn't dare take her eyes off the bear, even as it nosed at the jacket on the floor.

The window at the far end of the guesthouse was larger than the others, a rectangle of darkening sky framed by curtains torn and chewed by Marduk.

"Please, please let this work," Peyton whispered to herself. She could hear Marduk behind her, the sound of his heavy paws on the floor growing louder as he approached. Panic washed over her like an icy wave, and she knew she had to act fast.

With trembling fingers, she grasped the latch and fumbled with it, trying to force it open. As it finally gave way, she couldn't help but let out a small gasp of relief. But there was no time to celebrate; Marduk was almost upon her.

"Come on, come on," she muttered, frantically pushing the window open. With one last burst of adrenaline, she hoisted herself up and squeezed through the opening.

Just as she made it out, the sound of Marduk's snarl reached her ears. He lunged at the window, but she had pulled herself free just in time. Her heart pounded like a drum as she fell to the ground outside, landing hard on the damp earth.

For a moment, she lay there, catching her breath and trying to regain her bearings. Pain throbbed in her side from the fall, but she forced herself to stand.

Which way did Masterson go? she thought, scanning the dark landscape for any sign of him.

Her eyes darted around, finally catching sight of two men struggling nearby. One of them was Sean. The other man, someone she didn't recognize, seemed to be trying to hold him back.

"Sean!" Peyton shouted. She sprinted toward them, determined to put an end to the altercation and find Masterson before he could get away.

As she caught up to the two men, she grabbed the stranger's arm, twisting it forcefully behind his back. The man yelped in pain as he was pulled away from Sean.

"Where's Masterson?" Peyton demanded.

Sean's eyes blazed with anger, his chest heaving from the struggle. "I was following him until this idiot grabbed me!" He jerked his head toward the stranger.

"Hey, wait a minute," the man protested, wincing from Peyton's grip. "JM told me he was being framed! I was just trying to help!"

"Where is he now?" Peyton asked. She didn't care what lies Masterson might have told.

Before anyone could respond, the distant rumble of an engine starting up cut through the tense silence. Peyton's head whipped around, her gaze zeroing in on Masterson's house. A sleek truck roared down the road, its headlights piercing the falling darkness like twin beacons.

"That's him," she said, a sinking feeling in her stomach. "Has to be."

"Damn it!" Sean said, already running toward their car. "We need to catch up to him!"

But Peyton knew that by the time they reached their vehicle, Masterson would already be long gone. She scanned the area, desperately searching for another solution. As her eyes fell upon the hillside that led down to the road, an idea began to take shape.

"Wait, Sean!" she called out, putting her plan into action. "We can cut him off! Follow me!"

With no time to lose, Peyton sprinted down the hillside, her heart pounding in her chest as the roar of the truck's engine grew louder. Sean followed close behind, his breaths ragged from the exertion. The brush clawed at their clothes and skin, leaving shallow scratches as they plunged through the undergrowth.

As they burst onto the asphalt, Peyton saw the truck navigating a turn some distance away. She and Sean both drew their weapons, spreading their feet in the middle of the road as they waited.

But would he actually stop? There were too many ways for this to go wrong and end in injury or death.

As Masterson closed the distance, an alternative plan took shape in Peyton's mind—one that didn't involve bullets or standing in the path of an oncoming vehicle.

"Sean!" she yelled, gesturing to a dead, barkless tree standing precariously beside the road. "Help me push it over!"

Understanding her intentions, Sean holstered his weapon and joined her in rocking the lifeless trunk back and forth. Their combined strength strained against the stubborn timber, sweat dripping from their brows as they fought for leverage.

"He's going to get away!" Sean said, glancing nervously back at the approaching truck.

"Not if we keep pushing!" Peyton cried. Her muscles burned with effort, but she refused to give in, knowing that this was their best chance to stop Masterson.

With each heave, the tree teetered closer to the edge of collapse, its roots groaning in protest. Time seemed to slow as the truck bore down on them, its engine snarling like a predator closing in on its prey.

"NOW!" Peyton shouted, and together, they delivered one final, desperate push.

The tree gave way with a resounding crack, its splintered trunk plummeting to the ground just as Masterson's truck reached them. The headlights illuminated the fallen obstacle, and the screech of tires filled the air as he slammed on the brakes. But it was too late—the massive vehicle plowed into the tree with a deafening crunch of metal and wood.

For a moment, the world seemed to hold its breath, waiting for the aftermath to reveal itself.

"Come on," she muttered under her breath, her eyes never leaving the wreckage as she approached cautiously, her gun at the ready. The scent of burnt rubber and twisted metal hung heavy in the evening air.

" Risk, be careful!" Sean shouted after her, concern etched across his face. He followed closely behind, his own weapon gripped firmly in hand.

As Peyton neared the driver's side door, she caught sight of Masterson, dazed and disoriented, but seemingly unharmed. The airbag had absorbed the brunt of the impact, and he stared at her with a mixture of confusion and fear.

"What the hell is going on?" he asked, sounding a bit confused.

Peyton approached Masterson with her gun still drawn, then yanked the door of the truck open. "Get out of the vehicle slowly and put your hands behind your back."

Masterson stumbled out, still clearly disoriented. He held his hands up, but they shook slightly as he moved them behind his back. "I didn't do anything wrong," he protested weakly.

"No?" Peyton replied coldly, her eyes locked on his. "Then why did you try to get me killed?"

CHAPTER SEVENTEEN

Peyton handed Judd Masterson a bottle of water and a pair of pills, her eyes never leaving his face. "I hope these help with your headache," she said, masking her emotions behind a facade of professional concern.

"Thank you," Masterson murmured as he took the pills and chased them down with a gulp of water. The precinct interview room was devoid of any warmth or comfort—a place designed to make its occupants feel exposed and vulnerable. The only decoration was a two-way mirror, reflecting an image of the interrogator and suspect seated opposite each other, with Sean in the background, leaning against the wall.

Peyton studied Masterson closely as he leaned back in his chair, trying to gauge whether his disorientation was genuine or an act. He looked out of place in his white linen tunic that contrasted sharply with the austerity of the room. His expensive haircut did little to hide the tension in his jawline.

"Mr. Masterson," Peyton began, "why don't you start by telling us why you ran from us?"

Masterson stared at her, his brow furrowing with confusion. "I...I don't remember running," he admitted, rubbing his temple. "In fact, I remember very little from today. It's all fuzzy."

Peyton exchanged a glance with Sean, who arched an eyebrow, showing a skepticism that mirrored her own feelings. She refocused on Masterson and asked, "What's the last thing you remember, then?"

"Uh..." Masterson hesitated, his eyes scanning the ceiling as if searching for answers. "This morning, I was having coffee at my kitchen table, reading the newspaper." He paused, rubbing his forehead. "After that, it's all a blur. My head is aching so badly. You said I was in an accident, right? I think I must have a concussion."

Sean's face remained impassive, but Peyton could see the doubt in his eyes. The more she listened to Masterson, the more she became convinced he was faking his amnesia.

"Very convenient," Sean said. "First you run away, then you try to get your pet bear to eat my partner. Good thing you magically forgot about that, huh?"

Masterson's frown was a caricature of puzzlement. "What's this about a bear?"

"Where's Elisabeth Hall?" Peyton asked, cutting to the chase.

Masterson looked surprised by the question. "What do you mean?"

"Elisabeth went missing yesterday," Peyton said. "Nobody knows where she is. She's the third woman to go missing in Yellowstone in the past week, and the other two women both wound up dead. One of them was also your patient: Leticia Darrow."

Masterson's expression tightened as the gravity of the situation settled over him. "I...I don't know anything about what happened to those women," he insisted, a hint of fear creeping into his voice.

"Really?" Peyton asked, her dark eyes boring into him. "Because it seems like a hell of a coincidence that you were treating two of the victims—and then tried to run from us."

Masterson's face paled. His eyes darted around the stark interrogation room, as if searching for an escape from the situation he'd landed himself in. The dim light overhead cast eerie shadows on his face, making him look even more haunted and guilty.

"I swear," he said, his voice trembling, "I don't know anything about what happened to those women."

"Really?" Sean leaned forward, his eyes cold and unyielding. "What about Ernestine Johnson? Was she one of your patients, too?"

Masterson looked away, seeming to wilt under the intensity of Sean's gaze. He swallowed hard, his Adam's apple bobbing nervously. "Yes," he admitted quietly. "Ernestine was a client of mine. But I didn't do anything wrong. I haven't hurt any of them."

Peyton studied Masterson's face, searching for any hint of deception. She felt her heart clench with frustration, knowing that somewhere within this man might be the key to saving Elisabeth and avenging the other victims. But how could they crack his facade?

"Listen," she said, "here's what's going to happen. We're going to get a search warrant and scour every inch of your property. Your beautiful home, your office—everything. We'll dig up whatever secrets you've got hidden there."

Masterson's eyes widened, but he remained defiant. "You won't find anything. I'm innocent."

"Even if we don't find anything," Peyton pressed, leaning closer, "what will your other clients think when they learn you were counseling three women who have since gone missing, two of whom wound up dead? How many other young women will want you as their therapist after this?"

The room seemed to close in around Masterson, his pale face now slick with sweat. Fear clouded his eyes, and for a moment, Peyton thought she saw a flicker of remorse. But it vanished as quickly as it had appeared, leaving her to wonder if she'd imagined it.

"Look," Masterson whispered, his voice barely audible, "I didn't do anything wrong. I...I just want to help people."

"Then start by telling us the truth," Peyton said. "Why did you run?"

Masterson hesitated, his fingers nervously drumming on the cold metal table that separated them.

"Look," Sean said, "you're under suspicion for murder. You'd better start talking."

Masterson swallowed hard, a flicker of fear flashing across his eyes. He took a shaky breath and reluctantly began, "I...I got a little too close to some of my clients."

"Clarify," Peyton said, her patience wearing thin.

He looked away, embarrassed. "Things...got physical with some of the women."

Peyton felt a wave of disgust wash over her, her thoughts racing as she tried to comprehend how someone entrusted with helping vulnerable people could betray their trust so callously. It was monstrous.

"How could you take advantage of these women when they were coming to you with their problems?" she asked, her voice dripping with disdain. "They needed your help, and you used them for your own gratification."

"Wait!" Masterson's voice rose defensively, his eyes meeting hers once more. "It wasn't like that. I was just trying to comfort them, to make them feel better. I never meant for it to go too far."

"Comfort them?" Peyton asked, her mind reeling with images of the victims and the suffering they must have endured. "Sounds like a pretty selfish idea of comfort to me."

Peyton's stomach churned with a mix of anger and disgust as she stared at him. She needed to distance herself from him—she couldn't stomach another minute of his twisted justifications.

Sean seemed to understand the need to take over. He stepped forward and leaned both palms on the table, staring intently into Masterson's face.

"You're telling me," he said, "that you tried to kill my partner to protect your reputation?"

Masterson swallowed hard, his eyes darting to the side. "I panicked, okay? I thought if I could just distract you long enough to get away—"

"Distract us? By having a bear maul my partner?"

"He wasn't really going to kill her," Masterson said, his voice pleading now. "Marduk is intimidating, but he's harmless. I trained him that way. At most, he would've given your partner a few licks. That's all."

"And that's how you justify gambling with someone else's life," Sean said, shaking his head in disgust. "Where were you last night?"

Masterson hesitated for a moment, his eyes darting around the room as if searching for a way out. Then he cleared his throat and began to speak. "I was at a charity event downtown for most of the evening. After that, I went to a late dinner with some colleagues. We were at the restaurant until about midnight."

"Can anyone back that up?"

Masterson nodded. "Yes, I was with Dr. Thomas and Dr. Peterson. They can vouch for me. I'll give you their numbers, if you like."

"Good," Sean said. "We'll need to follow up with them to confirm your story."

"And then I can go free?"

Sean grunted. "Are you kidding me? You tried to serve my partner to a bear on a silver platter." He clenched his jaw, his eyes burning with anger. "You'll be seeing the inside of a prison for a while, if I have any say in the matter."

Masterson started to protest, but Sean ignored him and walked out. Peyton followed her partner, grateful for his support. He looked ready to throttle Masterson with his own hands, so angry was he for what had happened.

Outside the interrogation room, Peyton pondered what to do next. She felt betrayed by her own instincts, which had initially led her to suspect Masterson—but now, she couldn't help but question whether he truly was guilty.

"Are you okay?" Sean asked.

"Are you talking about the bear thing or what happened in there?" She gestured at the interview room.

"Both."

She sighed. "Well, the bear didn't do any real harm. I'm mostly just disgusted that he took advantage of those women." Her voice trembled with emotion, her thoughts consumed by the victims and their shattered trust. "They came to him for help, and he just...used them."

"I hear you," Sean said, his voice heavy with resignation. "Unfortunately, though, it sounds like he's probably innocent. I'm going to call to confirm his alibi, but my gut tells me Masterson is a creep, not a killer." He sighed, rubbing the back of his neck as if trying to relieve some tension.

Peyton clenched her jaw, frustrated by the turn of events. She wanted to believe there was still a chance they had their man, that it wasn't all for nothing. But she knew deep down that Sean was likely right—and that meant the real killer was still out there, free to strike again.

"Go ahead, make the call," she said, trying to push aside her anger and focus on what was most important: finding justice for the victims. They needed answers, and it seemed those answers would not be found within the confines of this interrogation room.

Peyton watched as Sean walked away down the desolate hallway. She felt an overwhelming sense of disappointment and disgust as she leaned against the cold wall, replaying the conversation with Masterson in her mind.

She closed her eyes, trying to envision the faces of the victims—women who had trusted Masterson with their deepest fears and secrets, only to be betrayed by him. It was a cruel twist of fate that he might not be the one responsible for their deaths after all.

"Damn it," she muttered under her breath. They were no closer to finding justice for these women, and the unknown killer was still out there, possibly stalking his next victim.

The sudden vibration of Peyton's phone in her pocket startled her back to the present. She quickly answered, hoping for some new piece of information that would give them a lead. "Risk here."

"Peyton, it's Peter Marshal. How are you holding up?"

"Trying our best here, but we just hit another dead end," she admitted, frustration evident in her voice. "Our suspect seems more like a predator than a murderer. Sean is checking his alibi now."

"Listen, there's been a new development," Marshal said gravely, causing Peyton's heart to drop. Fearing the worst, she braced herself for the news.

"Did they find Elisabeth?" she asked in a low voice.

"No, not yet," Marshal replied. "But another woman has gone missing. This time, though, we have witnesses."

CHAPTER EIGHTEEN

Charon's stomach was tumbling like a dryer as he steered the old SUV onto the dark, narrow logging road, his hands trembling on the wheel.

The night was an impenetrable black curtain, pierced only by the weak beams of his headlights. As he cut the engine and lights, the world outside became a void in which nothing existed except the distant, silvery stars.

His breath caught in his throat as he saw the flashing blue and red lights approaching in his rearview mirror. A police car roared past, its siren wailing like a banshee's cry before disappearing into the darkness. Charon exhaled, long and slow, feeling his pulse return to normal.

"Too close," he muttered under his breath, glancing nervously at the rearview mirror once more. His thoughts drifted back to the abduction, replaying the scene in his mind with a mixture of satisfaction and disbelief at how easily it had all gone.

The woman had been with a group of friends, eating ice cream with a group of friends outside a nature preserve. The sun had been setting, and the four friends had lounged in the sun's dying rays, oblivious to Charon's presence as he sat in his SUV in a nearby parking lot.

Charon had watched the woman from a distance, studying her movements and waiting for the opportune moment. He'd observed the way she brushed a stray lock of hair behind her ear, the way her eyes lit up when shc laughed at some joke shared with her friends.

Timing was everything. He knew that the key was to strike quickly, with enough force and confidence to leave everyone else stunned and hesitant to act. As she rose from her table, alone, to throw away her trash, Charon seized his chance.

"Hey, Alicia!" he called out, feigning familiarity. She turned toward him, a puzzled look on her face, no doubt trying to place him. That brief moment of hesitation was all he needed. In one swift movement, he closed the gap between them, gripped her arm tightly, and dragged her toward his SUV.

"Let go of me!" Alicia screamed, her voice shrill with panic. One of her friends shouted something, but they were too slow to realize what was going on, too slow to act. By the time they recognized the danger, it was too late.

With practiced ease, Charon shoved Alicia into the trunk and slammed the lid shut. The whole thing had taken mere seconds—time enough for him to slip away before Alicia's friends could catch up to them.

Despite the success of his mission, however, his nerves were frayed, a clear reminder of his distaste for mingling with society. He was an outsider, and sometimes he sensed that it was only a matter of time before his secrets were exposed.

Well, he thought, *I'd better go check on her, make sure she survived those potholes.*

He stepped out of the SUV, his boots crunching on gravel as he surveyed the desolate landscape. The moon cast an eerie glow over the dense forest that surrounded him, the air heavy with the scent of damp earth and decaying leaves. Silence permeated the night, broken only by the distant hooting of an owl and the drumming sound coming from the trunk.

"Damn it," Charon muttered under his breath, his irritation rising with each muffled thud. It was good to know she was alive, but even so, he had hoped she would be quiet for a while; but her fear, it seemed, was stronger than her common sense.

He walked around to the back of the vehicle, the drumming growing louder and more insistent. When he reached the trunk, he hesitated for a moment before finally opening it.

The young woman inside was a mass of tangled limbs, bound wrists, and disheveled hair. Her eyes were wide and glassy, their deep violet hue almost unnatural beneath the moonlight. They darted around, desperately searching for an escape route that didn't exist. A smattering of freckles framed her downturned mouth, giving her a doll-like appearance that both fascinated and repulsed Charon.

"Please," she whispered, her voice hoarse from screaming. "Please, let me go."

Charon sighed, bracing himself for the inevitable onslaught of pleas. It was always the same: the sobbing, the bargaining, the empty promises. He knew it was part of the process, but that didn't make it any less tedious.

"Please, I won't tell anyone," she continued, tears streaming down her cheeks. "I just want to go home."

"Quiet," Charon said, silencing her instantly. He watched her shiver uncontrollably for a moment, her fear a palpable entity in the confined space of the trunk.

After a few moments of thought, he made up his mind. "I'll make a deal with you," he said, his voice cold and measured. "If you can be good and do what I say, I'll let you sit in one of the seats. It's going to be a bumpy ride, so you'll be much happier there than in the trunk."

Her eyes widened at his words, and she nodded vigorously, eager for any small reprieve from her current nightmare. As she moved to climb out, Charon held up a hand, stopping her in her tracks.

"However," he continued, his tone icy, "if you try to escape or scream or otherwise cause problems, you'll go right back into the trunk. Do you understand?"

"Yes," she whispered. "I understand."

"Good," Charon said, stepping back and allowing her to scramble weakly out of the trunk. Her legs wobbled beneath her, unused to supporting her after hours spent curled up in the cramped space, but she managed to stay upright. Satisfied, Charon led her to the rear passenger door of the SUV and opened it, gesturing for her to enter.

As she climbed into the vehicle, she hesitated, her eyes catching sight of an intricately woven headdress lying on the seat. The feathers adorning it were long and vibrant, their colors reminiscent of deep tropical jungles and far-off exotic lands. Each plume seemed to shimmer as it caught the faint moonlight filtering through the trees.

"What is that?" she asked, nodding toward the headdress.

"Never mind that," Charon replied dismissively, a hint of impatience seeping into his tone. "It's for later." He didn't bother to elaborate, and the girl, sensing his growing irritation, quickly fell silent.

With a final glance at the headdress, she settled herself onto the seat, her body tense and her eyes darting nervously around the vehicle. Charon closed the door behind her, sealing her in the darkness with only the faint glow of the moon as her companion.

The moment the door clicked shut, sealing the girl inside, Charon felt a familiar thrill surge through his veins. He rounded the vehicle and slid into the driver's seat, his fingers gripping the wheel with an almost feverish intensity. With a practiced flick of his wrist, he ignited the engine, sending tremors coursing through the SUV's metallic frame.

As the headlights sliced through the inky blackness, Charon eased the vehicle back onto the road, leaving behind the desolate sanctuary of the logging trail. The scenery stretched out before him like a sea of shadows, the dense forest on either side of the winding road swallowing the weak glow of the moon. Skeletal branches clawed at the sky, while unseen creatures stirred within the undergrowth, their whispers carried away by the wind.

For a brief moment, the world beyond the car seemed to fall silent; even the girl in the backseat held her breath, as if she could somehow fade into the darkness and escape her fate. It was then that Charon rolled down his window, allowing the crisp night air to flood the vehicle. And with it came a sound that sent shivers down his spine: the haunting call of an owl ringing through the trees.

That mournful cry triggered something within Charon, a memory long buried beneath years of blood and pain. As a young boy, he had run from home and sought refuge in the wilderness, desperate to escape the misery that plagued his existence. Alone and afraid, he had wandered deeper into the woods until the world of man became nothing more than a distant memory.

It was there, amidst the towering pines and tangled roots, that he had received his vision. He remembered the way the shadows seemed to dance around him, forming grotesque shapes that taunted and tormented his fragile mind. And then, as if conjured from the very darkness itself, a figure had emerged before him. It was neither man nor beast, but something otherworldly—an ancient, primal force that whispered to him in a voice like the rustling of leaves.

"Your purpose is clear," it had hissed, its words weaving their way into Charon's soul. "You must cull the herd of humanity, remove the sick and weak, and feed them to the earth. Only then can the world be reborn, purified by the cleansing fires of death."

That vision had haunted him for years, shaping his every move until he became the instrument of destruction he was meant to be. Each life he took brought him closer to fulfilling his destiny; each sacrifice fed the insatiable hunger of the earth.

The woman's voice interrupted his thoughts. "Um...my name is Alicia," she said, her voice trembling slightly. "What's your name?"

"Charon," he replied curtly, his hands gripping the steering wheel tighter. He could feel her staring at him, seeking a connection or perhaps hoping to humanize herself in his eyes. It was useless; she was already marked for death.

"Charon? That's an unusual name," Alicia said.

"Charon is the ferryman who transports souls across the River Styx in Greek mythology," he explained, his voice devoid of emotion. "He serves as the guide for the dead, taking them from this world to the next. I chose the name because it represents my role—I, too, am a guide for the souls I claim."

A heavy silence settled over the SUV as Alicia absorbed his words. He could almost hear the cogs turning in her mind as she tried to make sense of her captor's perspective. Deep down, Charon reveled in the growing unease he had instilled within her.

"Are you going to kill me?" Alicia finally asked, her voice barely a whisper, as if saying it louder would make it more real.

"Yes," Charon answered without hesitation, his eyes locked on the road ahead. "But don't worry, you still have some time left." He glanced into the mirror, meeting her eyes with a smile. "Lucky for you, someone else is next in line."

CHAPTER NINETEEN

"He just came out of nowhere," Josh said, running a hand through his tousled brown hair. "By the time I knew what was happening, it was already too late."

Listening to Josh, Peyton felt bad for him. It was clear he felt responsible for Alicia's abduction, and yet it could have happened to anyone. The fact that the kidnapper had struck while Alicia was eating ice cream with three friends only underscored how bold and ruthless he was.

Peyton, Josh, and Sean stood at the side of a quiet road that ran adjacent to a nature preserve, its dense forest stretching as far as the eye could see. A worn wooden fence separated the road from the preserve, allowing only glimpses of the wild beauty within.

A few yards away, a lone picnic table stood beneath the shelter of an oak tree, its surface marred by spots of melted ice cream. The remnants of a once-happy gathering were scattered around it: discarded napkins, a crumpled soda can, and an empty ice cream container. As a gust of wind blew through the area, loose bits of trash danced around them, taunting reminders of the tragedy that had unfolded less than an hour before.

"Josh," Peyton said gently, "I know you're feeling guilty right now, but this isn't your fault. We'll do everything we can to find Alicia and bring her back safely." She paused, glancing at the picnic table and then back to him. "Do you remember anything else about the kidnapper? Anything that might help us identify him?"

He shook his head slowly, his eyes downcast. "I wish I could give you more, but it all happened so fast," he admitted, his voice cracking. "One moment we were laughing and eating ice cream, and the next...she was gone."

Peyton glanced at Sean, noticing in his eyes the same sympathy she herself felt. She turned back to Josh. "Were you two dating?" she asked, taking an educated guess.

He hesitated for a moment before nodding, his voice thick with emotion. "Yeah, we were. I always felt like it was my job to look out for her, you know? To protect her." He paused, swallowing hard. "And now...I couldn't even do that."

Sean cleared his throat. "Is there anyone you can think of who would want to harm Alicia? Any enemies or people she didn't get along with?"

Josh shook his head adamantly. "No. Alicia was...she was amazing. Everyone loved her. I can't imagine anyone wanting to hurt her."

"Alright," Peyton said, doing her best to keep her voice steady. "Can you describe the kidnapper for us? Anything you remember about him could help."

Josh squeezed his eyes shut as he tried to recall the details from the traumatic event. "He was big—maybe six feet or so? He wore a dark hoodie and jeans, but I couldn't see his face very well. It was all so fast..."

Before Peyton or Sean could ask a follow-up question, the sound of a car door clapping shut tore through the quiet evening air. Peyton's heart sank as she turned and noticed several dark sedans parked at the side of the road, their glossy exteriors reflecting the last remnants of the setting sun. Striding toward them with an unmistakable air of fury was Senator Joseph Hall, his face contorted in anger.

"Ranger Risk! How could you let another woman be kidnapped under your watch?" he demanded, not bothering to hide his frustration.

Sean stepped forward, trying to placate the irate senator. "Senator Hall, we're doing everything we can to catch the person responsible for these kidnappings—"

"Everything you can?" Hall interrupted, his voice rising in pitch. "And what progress have you made in finding my daughter, Elisabeth? Have you learned anything new at all?"

Peyton's jaw clenched as she fought to keep her own emotions in check. She knew the senator was simply worried about his daughter, but she couldn't help feeling a spark of resentment at his words nonetheless.

"We're exhausting every lead in our search for Elisabeth," she said, her voice measured and steady.

"Every lead? And yet you stand here, wasting time while my daughter is out there somewhere!" Senator Hall fumed, jabbing a finger at the horizon. "If you don't find her soon, I'll make sure you never work in law enforcement again!"

Desperate to calm the situation, Peyton spread her hands in a gesture of appeasement. "Senator, please understand that we're working around the clock to find your daughter and the other victims. We won't rest until they're brought home safely."

But her words seemed to fall on deaf ears. With a dismissive snort, Senator Hall stormed off toward his car, the door slamming shut with an unmistakable finality. Peyton watched as the senator was driven away, flanked by his two security vehicles, and then she exhaled a shaky breath.

"Peyton," Sean said quietly, placing a hand on her shoulder. "Don't take it personally. He's just a worried father who wants to see his daughter."

Peyton nodded. Returning her attention to Josh, she noticed his furrowed brow and clenched jaw. He had clearly been shaken by their conversation with the senator, and she found herself empathizing with his distress. The life of someone he cared about was in danger, and it was up to her and Sean to ensure a safe return.

"Hey," Josh said, swallowing hard. "Does that mean Alicia wasn't the only one kidnapped?"

"It seems that way," Sean replied. "But we're doing everything we can to find them both."

"Did you happen to notice the kidnapper's vehicle, by any chance?" Peyton asked, desperate for a new lead.

Josh hesitated, running a hand through his hair. "Yeah, I guess so. When I realized I couldn't catch up to the vehicle, I stopped to study it. It was a dark SUV—maybe a Ford Explorer or something similar. The paint was peeling off the hood, and there was a dent on the rear bumper."

"Good." Peyton nodded, making a mental note of the details. "What about the license plate?"

Josh shook his head, his eyes downcast. "No, I couldn't see it. It was obscured, like it had mud on it or something."

"Thank you, Josh," Peyton said, trying to keep a neutral expression on her face despite her disappointment. "You've been very helpful."

"Please find her," Josh whispered before he walked away to rejoin his two friends, who waited nearby. The group huddled together in a somber circle, their shoulders slumped and their faces etched with worry.

"Alright, I'm putting out an APB on that vehicle," Sean said, tapping away at his phone.

Peyton nodded, but her mind was elsewhere. She took in the scene once more: the nature preserve, its trees dark and foreboding in the fading light; the road that had carried Alicia and her kidnapper away; the picnic table, still bearing the remnants of melted ice cream, a testament to the innocence shattered moments ago.

As she stood there, Peyton tried to imagine how it all happened. Alicia and her friends laughing, enjoying their treats, unaware of the danger lurking nearby. The kidnapper, waiting patiently behind the cover of the trees or perhaps even in plain sight amongst the parked cars, biding his time until the perfect moment to strike.

Her instincts led her to the parking lot, where she studied the tire tracks, the spots of oil left behind by less-than-meticulous drivers, and the scattered bits of trash caught in the breeze. Where would the kidnapper have parked? Somewhere close enough for a quick getaway, but far enough to avoid arousing suspicion.

Peyton's eyes scanned back and forth as she mentally reconstructed the scene, her sharp intuition piecing together fragments of information. She imagined the kidnapper's vehicle tucked in the shadows, engine idling quietly, ready to spring into action.

A glimmer on the ground caught Peyton's eye as she walked among the parked cars. She bent down to get a better look, realizing it was a small feather. It was an iridescent shade of blue, with a delicate, almost ethereal quality. A few inches long, it seemed out of place among the dull colors and textures of the parking lot.

"We've got every cop within a hundred miles on the lookout for that vehicle," Sean said, putting away his phone as he joined her. He frowned as he studied the feather. "What's that?"

"Looks exotic, doesn't it? Like the one found at Leticia Darrow's crime scene."

"Similar, yeah," Sean agreed, rubbing his chin thoughtfully.

With a new sense of urgency, Peyton approached Josh and his two friends, who had been huddled together near the picnic table. One friend was a lanky young man with glasses and unruly hair, while the other was a petite girl with short, dark curls and an anxious expression.

"Josh," Peyton said, getting his attention. He turned toward her, his eyes still red-rimmed from earlier tears. "When you saw the kidnapper, did you notice him wearing anything unusual?"

Josh shook his head. "No, I just saw him from behind. I didn't even know he was there until he called to Alicia and grabbed her."

Disappointment settled in Peyton's chest, but she refused to give up. Turning to the other two friends, she asked, "Did either of you see someone watching you earlier? Anything suspicious at all?"

"Nothing," the girl replied, her voice trembling slightly. "I didn't even know something was wrong until Alicia screamed."

"Same here," the lanky young man added, his arms crossed defensively. "He just seemed to come out of nowhere."

Peyton frowned, thinking. "What exactly did the kidnapper say when he approached Alicia?"

Josh hesitated for a moment, his brow furrowing in concentration. "He...he called her name, and then he just...he just grabbed her."

A chill ran down Peyton's spine, her fingers tightening around the exotic feather she held. Could it be possible? She exchanged a meaningful glance with Sean, who seemed to grasp the gravity of what they'd just learned.

"He said her name?" she asked Josh. "You're sure?"

Josh nodded. "Positive." He blinked, not understanding. "He probably just heard one of us say her name."

"Maybe," Peyton said softly. "Or maybe he already knew her."

CHAPTER TWENTY

The fluorescent lights flickered overhead as Peyton and Sean strode through the bustling precinct. Uniformed officers rushed past, their faces a blur of determination and anxiety. Phones rang in staccato bursts, and the hum of activity filled the air.

"We need to cross-reference the description of the kidnapper's vehicle with people the victims knew," Peyton said to Sean. "If anyone the victims knew owned a dark Ford Explorer with peeling paint on the hood and a dented bumper, we might have our guy."

"Sounds a bit too easy," Sean said. "But it's worth a shot."

They arrived at a conference room tucked away in a corner of the precinct. Peyton closed the door behind them, sealing off the noise, and threw the blinds shut, ensuring privacy from prying eyes. She flipped open her laptop, its screen casting a pale glow on her determined face.

As Sean moved to fetch them both coffee, Peyton found herself thinking about Senator Hall's anger and threats to have them fired. The memory fueled her motivation to succeed, to prove him wrong about her abilities. She wasn't just some incompetent agent; she would find Elisabeth Hall and Alicia Doggart, and she would bring their kidnapper to justice.

She started her search with social media, focusing on the victims' profiles. Ernestine Johnson's page was filled with stunning landscape photographs and captivating stories of her journalistic adventures. Friends and family had left tearful messages, sharing heartfelt memories of her infectious laugh and unwavering determination.

Leticia Darrow's page was just as heartbreaking. Her husband, Gus, had left a long, heartbreaking tribute to her, describing what a wonderful wife and friend she was and how promising her future had been.

Elisabeth Hall's profile showcased an optimistic young woman who radiated positivity in the face of adversity. Well-wishers posted thoughts and prayers for her safe return, their words echoing Peyton's own hopes.

Lastly, Alicia Doggart's online presence painted a picture of a vibrant, outgoing woman who loved spending time with friends and exploring nature. Her most recent photo captured her bright smile as she held up a dripping ice cream cone. Comments flooded in, pleading for her safe return and offering comfort to her distraught family.

"Here's your coffee," Sean said, breaking through her focus as he entered the room and handed her a steaming cup.

"Thanks," Peyton replied, taking a sip of the strong brew before returning to her task. Sean took a seat at the table as well, his eyes locked on the screen of his laptop and his fingers typing furiously.

As Peyton dug deeper into the victims' connections, she stumbled upon a man named Isaiah Cunningham. Intrigued, she clicked on his profile and started reading about him.

"Sean, check this out," she said, turning her laptop toward him. "Isaiah Cunningham was friends with Ernestine, and he just so happens to drive a black Ford Explorer."

"Interesting," Sean said, leaning in to take a closer look. "What else do we know about him?"

"Let me see," Peyton said, pulling up the police database. She entered Cunningham's name, then tapped her fingers on the edge of the table as she waited for the results.

"Looks like he's got a criminal record," she said, leaning forward when the search had finished. "Petty theft, a couple of DUIs, and an assault charge from a bar fight four years ago."

She went back to social media and began searching through the pictures that Cunningham had set as public.

"His profile is full of pictures of him partying hard," she said, scrolling through the images. "Seems like a bit of a wild man."

She paused suddenly as she came across a video. "Oh no."

"What?" Sean asked, leaning closer.

Peyton's excitement dissipated in an instant, replaced by sinking disappointment as she clicked on the video, which had been posted just two days ago. The footage showed Isaiah dancing on a crowded beach, surrounded by friends and strangers alike. One of the tags read, 'Hermit Beach, Fort Lauderdale.' There were more recent videos, too, that made it clear Cunningham was still there.

"Damn, he's been in Florida all week," Peyton muttered, slumping back in her chair. "It couldn't have been him."

"Well, that sucks," Sean said. He sighed. "Back to the drawing board, I guess."

Peyton, however, needed to give her mind a break. She rose and began pacing along the table. As she did so, she tried to piece together a coherent pattern, something that might reveal the killer's motive—but it was like trying to complete a puzzle with only half the pieces.

"Think, Peyton, think," she whispered under her breath, her eyes flicking over to Sean, who was equally absorbed in his work. The weight of responsibility bore down on her; Elisabeth's and Alicia's lives were in their hands, and they couldn't afford any missteps.

"Maybe we're looking at this all wrong," she murmured, pausing her pacing for a moment. "What if the connection isn't through mutual friends or shared interests? What if it's something deeper, more personal?" She tapped her finger against her chin, her mind grappling with the possibilities.

Deciding she needed to focus more exclusively on the latest victim, she sat down again and dove into Alicia's online presence. She soon discovered that the young woman had a passion for painting landscapes and volunteering at a local animal shelter. Apparently, she had been studying environmental science at university before her sudden disappearance.

As Peyton continued to scroll through Alicia's posts, one detail caught her eye.

"Sean," she said. "Listen to this. Alicia has idiopathic pulmonary fibrosis. It's a rare lung disease that causes scarring of the lungs, making it difficult to breathe. It looks like she's been dealing with it for years, but it's been getting worse."

"Could that have something to do with why she was targeted?" Sean asked, his eyes narrowing as he considered the implications.

"Maybe. I'm not sure how it fits yet, but there must be a reason why the killer chose these specific victims."

Sean's fingers flew across his keyboard, the rhythmic tapping a counterpoint to the hum of fluorescent lights above them. Peyton watched him for a moment before returning her gaze to her own laptop. Her mind was still reeling from the discovery of Alicia's health condition. Could it be the key to understanding why she and the others had been targeted?

"Peyton," Sean said suddenly, breaking her concentration. "I just found something interesting. Ernestine had a health condition, too. She had multiple sclerosis."

"Really?" Peyton's eyes widened as the pieces began to fit together in her mind. "Wait a minute...Elisabeth suffers from scleroderma, doesn't she? And Judd Masterson's wife..." She paused, frowning.

"She was depressed," Sean said. "It's not the same kind of condition exactly, but—"

"But it is a malady of sorts," Peyton finished.

Sean nodded. "So all four victims had some sort of serious health issue. It can't be a coincidence."

"Definitely not." Her heart pounded with excitement. This could be the breakthrough they needed.

As they dug deeper into the victims' medical histories, Peyton noticed a name that kept coming up: Guardian Health Services. She clicked on their website and discovered that GHS was a nationwide healthcare provider that specialized in treating patients with chronic illnesses.

Looking more carefully through the victims' profiles, she found mentions of GHS among all the victims, suggesting that all four had been using the service.

"That's it," Peyton said softly, stunned.

"What's it?" Sean asked.

"The common link. It's healthcare, Sean—and more specifically, GHS."

"You think the killer's got a grudge against GHS?"

"Either that," Peyton said, her voice fervent with conviction, "or he's just using the company to identify and target vulnerable individuals. He could be on staff there or have some kind of access to their database."

"Whatever the case," Sean said grimly, "we've got to stop him ASAP. GHS is a big organization, so I doubt he'll be running out of targets any time soon."

CHAPTER TWENTY ONE

"Thank you for calling Guardian Health Services," a prerecorded voice announced over the speaker. "For billing inquiries, press one. For scheduling appointments, press two. For medical records, press three."

Peyton's finger jabbed the number three with impatience, eager to get through to someone. She couldn't shake the feeling that the lives of Elisabeth and Alicia were slipping further away with every passing second.

"Please hold while we connect you to a representative," the recording droned on.

As the seconds ticked by, Peyton could feel the tension mounting in the room. She tapped her foot nervously, her mind racing with possibilities and what-ifs. Finally, after what felt like an eternity, a woman's voice came through the line.

"Hello, this is Diana speaking. How may I help you today?" The woman's tone was friendly, but there was an unmistakable hint of weariness in her voice, as if she were nearing the end of her shift and ready to go home.

"Hi, Diana. My name is Ranger Peyton Risk with the National Park Service. I'm investigating a series of homicides and kidnappings, and it seems that all the victims had one thing in common: they were using GHS for their healthcare."

Diana's surprise was evident in her voice. "Oh my...that's... I mean, I don't even know what to say. That's terrible."

"Right now, I just need access to the patient records of four specific women. Time is critical, and any information you can provide could help save lives." Peyton's eyes locked onto Sean's, silently communicating the importance of what they were doing.

"Ranger Risk, I understand the urgency of your situation, but I'm afraid I can't provide you with that information," Diana said, a hint of apology in her voice. "It's against company protocol, and I could lose my job if I were to give out patient records without proper authorization."

"Please, Diana," Peyton said. "Lives are at stake here. We may be able to prevent more people from getting hurt if we can find out who's targeting these women. You have the power to help us."

There was a brief pause on the other end, and Peyton could hear Diana taking a deep breath before responding. "I'm truly sorry, but my hands are tied in this matter. I wish I could help you, but there's nothing I can do."

"I understand," Peyton said in a hollow voice. "Thank you for your time."

"Of course. Best of luck."

"Damn it," Peyton muttered under her breath as she hung up the phone. She clenched her fists, trying to suppress the anger and frustration bubbling within her.

"Anything?" Sean asked, his eyebrows furrowing in concern.

"Nothing. They won't release the records." Peyton's jaw tightened as she stared at the blank screen of her phone, her mind racing with possible courses of action.

Sean hesitated for a moment before suggesting, "We could get a search warrant to look at those records. I know where the company's headquarters is located."

Peyton shook her head, her dark hair falling into her eyes. "We don't have time for that. Every second counts, and going through the legal process could take days. We need to act now."

Then she had an idea. Her eyes met Sean's again, determination burning within them. "How far exactly is their headquarters?"

***

"Are you sure about this?" Sean asked as they pulled up to GHS headquarters, a modern structure with sleek, reflective glass windows that were now shrouded in darkness. The area surrounding the headquarters was equally desolate, with only a few streetlights offering any illumination.

"Breaking in there," Sean added. "I get the urgency, but this is definitely crossing a line."

Peyton's eyes were fixed on the building. "I know it's not ideal, but we need those records, Sean. If you can't handle this, you can stay here. I'll do it myself."

Sean frowned, his eyes clouded with concern. "Peyton, this is the kind of thing that got you kicked out of the FBI in the first place. I don't want to see you throw away everything you've worked for."

"Sometimes rules have to be broken to save lives," Peyton argued. "If something happens to those women, won't you wish you'd done something?"

Sean said nothing.

"Look," she said, "I'm doing this with or without you. You can stay back if your conscience can't handle it."

Tired of waiting, she stepped out of the car. The GHS headquarters loomed before her, a modern concrete and glass monolith surrounded by tall trees and a high fence. The shadows cast by the moonlight gave the place an eerie, almost sinister appearance, but Peyton's determination to uncover the truth burned brighter than any fear. She knew that within those walls, the information they needed to break open this case was waiting.

As she approached the building and began searching for a way in, she noticed a side door tucked away in a shadowy alcove. It was the perfect spot to attempt entry. She pulled a pair of bobby pins from her hair, bending them with practiced ease into makeshift lock picks. She inserted them into the keyhole, holding her breath as she attempted to manipulate the tumblers inside. Her fingers were trembling slightly, making it difficult to finesse the delicate tools.

"Damn it," she muttered under her breath, frustration mounting as the lock refused to yield.

"Here," Sean said softly as he appeared beside her, holding out a small toolkit. "I always carry these with me, just in case."

Peyton nodded, grateful for his help. She rummaged through the toolkit until she found a lock pick set, selecting a slender tool with a curved tip. She inserted it into the lock, her fingers working deftly as she manipulated the pins. After a few tense moments, she heard a satisfying click, and the door swung open.

Sean looked at her with a mixture of awe and concern. "I can't believe you did that. You're like some kind of spy."

Peyton grinned at him. "Aren't you glad you came along?"

Joking aside, she felt grateful for his presence. He had chosen to join her, despite his reservations, and that meant everything to her.

The darkness inside GHS headquarters was oppressive, the air thick with tension as Peyton and Sean slipped through the door. The only source of light came from the faint glow of emergency exit signs. They moved cautiously, their footsteps muffled by plush carpeting.

"Where do you think they'd keep the patient records?" Sean asked in a hushed tone, sticking close to Peyton.

"Probably in an office or secure room," she replied, her eyes scanning the dimly lit space for any clues. As an investigator, Peyton had honed her intuition over the years, and it was now guiding her forward, down a long hallway lined with closed doors.

As they progressed, Peyton's thoughts turned inward. If she could just find the connection between the four victims, it might help prevent more tragedies. But time was running out, and they were taking a massive risk being here without a warrant. What would happen if they were caught?

Rounding a corner, Peyton noticed a thin sliver of light seeping out from beneath one of the doors. Her heart raced as she approached, drawn by the promise of information that lay within. Peering through a window, she saw a computer on a cluttered desk, surrounded by filing cabinets.

"Looks like we found an office," she whispered to Sean, who nodded. "Let's check it out."

Peyton rounded a corner and was about to head toward the door when Sean grabbed her arm and yanked her back. Confused and startled, she looked up at him, about to protest, when he pointed silently to the corner of the ceiling. There, mounted unobtrusively, was a security camera, its red light blinking menacingly.

"Shit," she murmured, her heartbeat pounding in her ears. They'd come so close to getting caught. She shot Sean a grateful look and mouthed the words, "Thank you."

They retreated back down the hallway, looking for another way into the office that would avoid the camera's watchful gaze. After a few tense moments, they found a service door that led to a storage room adjacent to the office.

Creeping into the office through the connecting door, Peyton's eyes took in her surroundings. The room was compact, filled with a chaotic blend of file cabinets, overflowing shelves, and stacks of paper strewn across every surface. A single desk sat near the back of the room, its surface obscured by an avalanche of forms and folders. It was a far cry from the sterile, organized workspace she'd grown accustomed to during her time at the FBI.

"Let's see what this computer can tell us," she whispered to Sean.

She approached the desk, careful not to disturb anything that might give away their presence. In the dim light seeping in through the blinds, she could make out the outline of the keyboard and monitor. With a quick prayer, she pressed the power button.

The computer whirred to life, the hum of the fan accompanying the faint glow of the screen as it blinked awake. "Come on," she muttered under her breath, tapping her fingers impatiently against the desk. As the login screen appeared, her heart sank—she'd need a password.

"Damn it," she hissed, her frustration mounting. She tried a few generic passwords—'password123', 'admin', even 'GHS'. Each attempt was met with the same disheartening result: 'Incorrect Password'.

"Peyton." Sean's urgent whisper cut through her thoughts, causing her to jump slightly. He was peering through the blinds at something outside. "There's a car pulling up. We might've tripped an alarm."

"Shit," she muttered, panic rising in her chest. They were running out of time. She took a deep breath, trying to calm her racing mind.

Her eyes darted around the office, searching for a clue that might help her guess the password. In desperation, she turned her attention to the desk itself. Amidst a pile of papers and a coffee-stained mug was a framed photograph of a smiling family: a man, a woman, and two young children. An idea struck her like a bolt of lightning—perhaps it was as simple as the name of one of the family members.

But who were they?

She turned the frame over and saw a handwritten note scrawled on the back. It read, "To my loving husband, Jason, and our two beautiful children, Emily and Ethan. Love always, Sarah." Below this was the date: 10/21/2015.

Peyton 'Sarah' as the password. No dice. Then, thinking on her feet, she added the numbers at the end: 'Sarah10212015.' Still nothing.

"Come on," she muttered.

Finally, she tried something a bit simpler than the last one: 'Sarah2015.' The screen flashed, and she was granted access. Relief flooded through her as she quickly navigated the computer's files.

"Got it!" she exclaimed, finding the records she'd been searching for. Her eyes skimmed the records on the four victims with practiced speed, committing every detail to memory.

"Peyton, we've got to go," Sean said, his tone anxious as he continued to keep watch at the window. The sound of approaching footsteps were growing louder by the second.

"Almost done," she murmured, her heart hammering in her chest. She knew they were cutting it close, but she couldn't leave without the information they needed. It was now or never.

"Peyton, come on!" Sean urged in a hushed tone, glancing nervously back at the door.

Just then, she spotted a name that stood out among the files: Edgar Graves. He was the case manager for all four victims. He had to be the link they were looking for. Without wasting another second, she committed his name to memory, closed the files, and turned off the computer.

"Let's go," she whispered, following Sean as he crept toward the door. They could hear the footsteps growing louder, closer. A sudden rush of adrenaline coursed through her veins.

As they reached the door, they paused, pressing themselves against the wall. The footsteps stopped right outside the office, and the sound of a key sliding into the lock filled the tense silence. Peyton held her breath, fear and anticipation knotting in her stomach.

"Quick, this way," Sean mouthed, his eyes wide with urgency. He led her back to the door they'd used to first enter the room. The door opened with a soft creak.

They slipped inside, careful not to make a sound. The door clicked shut just as the sound of the main office door swung open. Peyton's heart hammered in her chest, but she couldn't help feeling a rush of satisfaction at the same time.

"Edgar Graves," she said under her breath, repeating the name like a mantra. "We've got something now."

"Let's get out of here first," Sean replied, his voice barely audible. Carefully, they made their way down the hallway, avoiding any creaking floorboards and staying in the shadows.

Finally, they reached a back exit. Sean cracked the door open just enough to check for any guards or cameras before giving Peyton a nod. They slipped out into the cool night air, their breath visible in the darkness.

"Come on," Peyton whispered. Together, they sprinted to their car parked a safe distance away from the building. As they climbed inside, Peyton couldn't suppress a smile of triumph.

"Edgar Graves," she repeated once more, feeling a renewed sense of hope. "We've got something to work with now."

"Let's hope it's enough," Sean replied, starting the engine. The car pulled away, leaving Guardian Health Services behind them, but carrying the thread that could unravel the mystery they'd been chasing.

CHAPTER TWENTY TWO

Elisabeth's fists slammed against the wooden bars of the cage, her voice raw from screaming for help. She slumped back, exhausted, the rough floor digging into her spine.

It was useless—there was no breaking out.

In this cramped prison, she couldn't even stretch out her legs. Her heart raced as her mind conjured images of Charon's twisted face—his cold eyes and sneering grin haunting her thoughts.

"Please," she whispered, tears streaming down her cheeks, "Somebody...help me."

As if mocking her, the memory of earlier that evening played in her mind. She had been so close to freedom. The wind on her face, her muscles working tirelessly in a desperate sprint for safety. She'd seen two ATVs zipping past like a lifeline within reach, and she had screamed at the top of her lungs for them to stop. But they hadn't heard her; the roar of their engines had drowned out her cries.

Charon, however, had heard her all too well. His hand clamped around her arm like a vice, wrenching her back into his world of horror. The terror she'd felt in that moment had been palpable, an icy grip on her already weakened heart.

Her optimism, usually her guiding light in life, flickered in the suffocating darkness. Her breath came in short gasps, her chest tightening with the crushing weight of claustrophobia and fear. The oppressive darkness of the blanket over the cage seemed to seep into her very soul. That blanket was her punishment for running—now she would be forced to sit in complete darkness, right up until it was time for her to be 'sacrificed.'

"Your time will come soon," Charon had sneered before leaving her in this nightmarish prison. His threat echoed in Elisabeth's mind, fueling her dread. She couldn't see a thing within the confines of her wooden cage, but she could feel the rough, splintered bars beneath her fingertips as she tried to find any weakness in her prison.

As she cowered there, every creak and groan from the building set off a fresh surge of panic. When she heard what sounded like footsteps outside, she froze, her pulse racing. After a moment, she realized it was just the wind, moaning through the hidden gaps in the structure around her.

She knew she was in some sort of building; after Charon had recaptured her, he'd thrown her back into the cage and loaded it into a vehicle. He drove for what felt like an eternity before stopping, then clumsily hauled her cage out, dropping it onto the ground with a jarring thud. Her body cried out in pain, but she bit her lip, refusing to give him the satisfaction of hearing her suffer.

"Please," Elisabeth whispered, her voice barely audible even to herself. "Please let me find a way out of here."

She knew that when Charon returned, he wouldn't hesitate to kill her. Desperation flooded through her veins, spurring her into action.

"Come on, Elisabeth, you have to find a way out," she whispered to herself, focusing on the task at hand. Her hands trembled as she carefully felt around the wooden cage, her fingers searching for any flaw or weakness.

Her fingertips grazed against something unexpected—a jagged edge where one of the wooden bars had splintered when the cage fell. Hope surged within her; if she could break the bar the rest of the way, she might be able to squeeze through the gap.

"Please, let this work," she prayed softly, positioning herself to apply as much force as possible to the weakened bar. With a determined grunt, she threw her weight against it, feeling the cracked wood give slightly under the pressure. Again and again, she rammed herself into the bar until, finally, it snapped with a satisfying crack.

"Thank God," she breathed. The gap left by the broken bar was still uncomfortably tight, but she knew it might be her only chance at freedom. Taking a deep breath, she began to wriggle her way through the opening, her body protesting with each strained movement.

As she squeezed herself through the gap, the heavy blanket covering the cage shifted, allowing slivers of moonlight to filter in through the windows. Elisabeth gasped at the sudden brightness, her eyes struggling to adjust after being engulfed in darkness for so long.

Once she had managed to free herself from the cage, she took a moment to survey her surroundings. The small room she found herself in appeared to be some kind of storage space, filled with old furniture draped in dusty sheets. Cobwebs clung to the corners of the room, and the air was musty with disuse.

"Okay, Elisabeth," she told herself, her voice shaking. "You've made it this far. Now, you just need to find a way out before Charon comes back."

She took one last glance at the wooden cage that had held her captive, its broken bar a testament to her determination. Her heart swelled with hope, but she knew there was no time for celebration. She had to get out right away, before–

Just then, the piercing glare of headlights cut through the darkness outside. The sudden sound of a vehicle approaching sent her into a frantic frenzy. Like a cornered animal, she dashed across the room and locked the door.

"Please," she whispered to herself, her hands trembling against the cold metal doorknob. "Please let this be enough."

As the car door slammed shut, Elisabeth's breath hitched. She pressed her back against the door, praying it would hold.

The footsteps paused. The door rattled gently, then more fiercely.

"Elisabeth!" Charon roared from the other side. The door shook as he tried to force it open. His fists pounded against the wood like a violent drumbeat. "Open the damn door!"

Never, she thought, choking back a sob. But her defiance was silent; she couldn't bring herself to speak.

"Elisabeth, I swear if you don't open this door—" Charon's voice broke off, leaving a chilling silence. For a moment, she dared to believe that he might have given up.

Then the door shook, throwing her back. He must have kicked the door. The blow came again, and this time it was followed by a sound that caused Elisabeth's heart to skip a beat.

The sound of splintering wood.

CHAPTER TWENTY THREE

"What is he doing?" Peyton wondered aloud, watching the man – Edgar Graves, she presumed – pacing back and forth within his house. He moved with an anxious energy, his hands running through his hair and his head shaking occasionally.

Glancing at the illuminated clock on the dashboard, Sean frowned.

"Almost one o'clock," he muttered. "Awfully late to be up."

They were parked on a crowded street in a quiet neighborhood. They had been sitting there for the past fifteen minutes, watching the figure through the windows of his house. As far as Peyton could tell, he was alone, but she didn't want to make any assumptions. For all she knew, Elisabeth and Alicia could be locked in his basement.

"I think we've waited long enough," she said. "If he was going to lead us to the victims, he would've done so already."

She unbuckled her seat belt and reached for the door handle. Before she could pull it, however, Sean's hand shot out and grasped her wrist gently.

"Hey," he said. "Be careful, alright? I know I've been overprotective before, but this feels...off. If things go sideways, don't try to be the hero."

A soft smile crossed her lips as she looked into his eyes, understanding the weight of his concern. "I won't if you won't," she said.

"Deal," he agreed with a nod, releasing her wrist.

As Peyton stepped out of the car, the damp night air clung to her, the scent of rain still lingering from earlier. They approached the house cautiously, taking in the details of its exterior. It was a two-story building with dark bricks and contrasting white trim around the windows. Ivy climbed up one side, adding an air of age to the otherwise modern structure. The front yard bore signs of meticulous care: each shrub trimmed to perfection, the walkway lined with neatly arranged flowers.

Peyton knocked on the front door. The sound carried sharply across the quiet street, but no answer came from within the house. The silence weighed heavily upon her, her intuition whispering that something was amiss.

As she reached for the handle to knock again, she heard a scream from within the house. Wasting no time, Sean drew his weapon and kicked the door open with a resounding crash. Peyton's heart raced as she followed suit, drawing her own weapon and stepping into the entryway.

"Stay close," Sean whispered. They moved cautiously, their weapons at the ready, searching for the source of the scream.

"Help!" came another scream, louder this time, and more desperate. Peyton realized it was coming from upstairs. She was closer to it than Sean was, so she went first before he could protest.

As Peyton ascended the staircase, her muscles tensed with anticipation. Every creak underfoot caused her to clench her teeth hard.

Reaching the top of the stairs, she paused, catching her breath. The house seemed to hold its breath with her, waiting for her next move.

The upstairs was dark, with shadows pooling in the corners and creeping along the walls. The wallpaper was faded, its once-vibrant pattern now just a dull echo of its former glory.

Peyton moved slowly down the hallway, her footsteps muffled by the worn carpet beneath her feet. Every nerve in her body felt raw and exposed, anticipation crackling through her like static electricity.

As she approached a partially-open door at the end of the hall, the murmur of conversation reached her ears. Her grip on the gun tightened, sweat prickling at the base of her neck. She hesitated for just a moment before pushing the door open and stepping inside.

The room was dominated by a large TV that flickered with images of terror and violence. Peyton's eyes widened as she took in the gruesome scenes playing out on the screen, the colors of blood and darkness painting the room in a macabre tableau. With a sinking feeling, she realized the screams she'd heard were not those of a victim in peril, but merely the chilling soundtrack of a horror movie.

Something struck the ground behind her. She turned around to see a bowl of popcorn lying on the floor, the pieces scattered about. Above it stood a man in his forties, with salt-and-pepper hair that framed a face lined with age and worry. His eyes, gray as a storm-tossed sea, regarded her with a mix of curiosity and apprehension.

"Edgar Graves?" Peyton asked, trying to keep her voice steady despite the adrenaline coursing through her veins.

"Peyton, are you okay?" Sean called as he approached down the hall. He paused a few paces behind the man, his presence like a reassuring anchor in the storm of emotions that threatened to engulf Peyton.

"I'm fine," she said, never taking her eyes off the man before her.

"Would someone mind telling me what's going on?" the man asked, looking puzzled as he stared at the spilled popcorn.

"Sorry for barging in like this, Mr. Graves," Peyton said, her heart still pounding from the earlier adrenaline rush. "We're investigating a case, and we need to ask you some questions. Mind explaining what you're doing up so late?"

"Couldn't sleep," he replied, rubbing the back of his neck. "I've had a long, difficult day dealing with clients and paperwork. I thought watching a movie might help me relax." He glanced at their weapons, then back at their faces. "Would you mind putting those away? It's not every day someone breaks into your home armed."

Hesitantly, Peyton lowered her weapon, feeling slightly foolish. Sean followed suit, but she could sense his lingering wariness.

"Is there anyone else in the house?" Sean asked.

"No, I live alone," Graves said. "What is this about exactly?"

"Where were you yesterday evening?" Peyton asked.

"I was on a business trip," he replied without hesitation.

"A business trip?"

Seeing the doubt flicker in Peyton's eyes, Graves walked over to a nearby desk, rifling through a stack of papers before producing a set of plane ticket stubs. "Here, these should prove I was gone. I only got back earlier this evening."

At first, it puzzled Peyton how quickly Graves produced the proof. Then, recalling that he worked in health insurance, it occurred to her that he was used to furnishing documentation.

"Can you tell us what the business trip was about? What did you do there?" Peyton asked, examining the ticket stubs.

"Sure," Graves said, clearly eager to put their doubts to rest. "I went to meet with some potential new clients for Guardian Health Services. We discussed insurance plans, pricing, and services offered. It wasn't anything out of the ordinary."

Peyton tried to read him, searching for any signs of deception, but his face remained open and honest. Could this really be a dead end?

"Thank you, Mr. Graves," she said finally, handing back the ticket stubs. "We appreciate your cooperation."

"Is there anything else I can help you with?" he asked, his tone softening slightly as he noticed their sagging shoulders.

"No, I think we have what we need for now," Peyton said, trying to hide her disappointment. "Again, we apologize for the intrusion."

With that, Peyton and Sean made their way out of the room, leaving Edgar Graves and his spilled popcorn behind. They had only gone halfway down the stairs, however, when his voice reached them.

"Are you two looking for Charlie, by any chance?"

"Charlie?" Sean asked, eyebrows furrowed as he twisted back to look up the stairs at Graves, who stood at the top.

"Charlie Addison," Graves said with a sigh. "He was the case manager before me. Got fired for making some bizarre comments to clients."

"Bizarre comments?" Peyton asked.

"He'd tell them weird things, like how important it was for the 'herd of humanity' to be kept healthy, and how sometimes that meant 'culling the sick'—stuff like that. It really unsettled people."

Peyton exchanged a glance with Sean, who seemed equally intrigued. "Where can we find this Charlie?" she asked.

Graves hesitated for a moment, as if weighing whether or not to divulge the information.

"We just want to talk to him," Sean said. "This isn't a witch hunt."

Graves nodded. "He lives on the east side of town—in a small, green house off Elm Street. But last I heard from him, he had a job that involved working strange hours."

He raised his hands as if to ward off an accusation. "I know, I know. Why would I keep in touch with a guy like that? He helped me transition into my role at GHS, alright? I felt I owed him something, and it was pretty clear he needed a friend—not that he necessarily *wanted* one."

"What kind of work does he do?" Peyton asked.

"From what he told me, he spends most of his time at the park, collecting soil samples."

"The park?" Sean asked.

Graves nodded. "Yellowstone. Where else?"

CHAPTER TWENTY FOUR

Peyton peered through the window and into the dark interior of the ranger station, straining her eyes. It was hard to make out any details; all she could see were vague outlines of furniture and walls. She pressed her forehead closer to the glass, attempting to decipher any signs of life within.

Earlier, she and Sean had decided to split up—he went to Charlie Addison's house while she ventured back to Yellowstone in search of the elusive scientist. Since she didn't know where Addison would be working in the vast expanse of the park, she had come to Dave Turner's ranger station for help. But now, she faced another problem: She didn't know if Dave was even here or if he had left his post.

"Come on, Dave," she whispered under her breath as she knocked again, praying that someone would respond.

Seconds passed in silence. Then, to Peyton's relief, she heard shuffling noises as a figure emerged from the dimness of the station. The door opened, revealing a haggard-looking Dave Turner rubbing his eyes.

Dave squinted at her, surprise registering on his face when recognition dawned.

"Peyton?" he asked, his voice hoarse. "Come in, come in."

As Peyton stepped into the ranger station, Dave flicked on a light, casting a warm glow across the room. The sudden brightness made her squint, and she blinked to adjust her eyes.

"What can I help you with?" Dave asked, concern furrowing his brow. "Must be important for you to show up at..." He checked his watch. "Just past two in the morning." There was surprise in his voice, but no hint of reproach. He seemed too good-natured for that.

"I'm looking for a man named Charlie Addison," she said, studying his face for any sign of recognition. "Do you know him?"

Dave's eyes narrowed as he thought. After a moment, he shook his head slowly. "No, I don't think so. Why would he be in Yellowstone?"

"Charlie studies soil samples," she said, trying not to be disappointed. She had hoped Dave would know him. If Dave couldn't help her, what would she do? How was she supposed to find Charlie in such a massive park—and without him knowing she was looking for him?

"Wait a minute..." Dave said, moving over to his desk. He leaned against it, searching through the cluttered surface. "I ran into a team of scientists studying soil samples just the other day."

"Really?" Peyton's voice was a mix of excitement and caution. This could be the lead she needed. "What were they doing?"

"Taking samples of the soil and testing for different properties," Dave said, his voice trailing off for a moment as he dug through a stack of papers.

"Where did you see them?" she asked.

A soft rustle of papers filled the dim room as Dave rummaged through his desk, finally pulling out a small, battered journal. "I keep track of my daily activities and observations in this," he explained, flipping through the pages until he found the right entry.

Peyton shifted her weight from one foot to another, doing her best to be patient.

"Ah, here it is," Dave said quietly, reading the passage to himself. His brow furrowed in concentration as he parsed the details in his own handwriting. "According to this, the scientists I saw were working in the northeastern area of Yellowstone. The location is called Starlight Canyon."

"Starlight Canyon," Peyton said, her mind racing to memorize the name. "How do I get there?"

Dave hesitated for a moment. "I could take you there myself, if you wanted."

"Thank you, but you're still recovering," she replied, glancing at the neck brace encircling his throat. She couldn't bring herself to put him in danger. "Just tell me how to get there, and I'll manage on my own."

"Suit yourself." He traced a route on his map, describing the turns and landmarks she needed to follow. "It's going to be difficult navigating the trails in the dark, though. You'll need to watch your step and keep an eye out for wildlife."

"I will," Peyton said, nodding. Dave handed her the map, and she pocketed it. "Thank you, Dave. I can't tell you how helpful you've been."

Dave dug a set of ATV keys from his pocket and handed them to her. "You'll find the ATV in the shed out back, same as before," he said, concern furrowing his brow. "And please, be careful?"

"I'll return it to you in one piece."

He grunted. "I wasn't talking about the ATV."

She smiled. She hadn't known him long, but he was growing on her quickly.

"I will," she said. "Now go back to sleep."

He made a mock salute. "Yes, ma'am."

Still smiling, Peyton retreated and stepped outside. As she did so, the darkness seemed to swallow her whole. She headed toward the shed with determined strides, her breath forming ghostly puffs in front of her face.

Just as she reached out to open the door to the shed, her phone vibrated in her pocket, startling her. Fishing it out, she saw Sean's name on the screen and quickly answered.

"Peyton," Sean said without preamble, his voice tense and slightly breathless, "I'm at Charlie Addison's place. There's no sign of him or anyone else here. Have you had any luck?"

"Actually, yes," she said. "Dave mentioned a group of scientists studying soil samples in Starlight Canyon. He thinks that might be where they are."

"Starlight Canyon? That's pretty remote." Concern laced Sean's voice. "It won't be easy getting there, especially at night."

"Dave gave me directions, and I'm taking an ATV," she said. "I can handle it. Just meet me there as soon as you can."

"Alright." Sean hesitated for a moment before adding, "Stay safe, Peyton. I'll see you soon."

"See you soon," she echoed, and ended the call. She pulled the shed door open and was relieved to see the familiar shape of the ATV in the dim light. She quickly climbed on and started the ignition, the engine roaring to life. As she drove away from the cabin, she felt a sense of apprehension creeping up her spine. What if Charlie wasn't in Starlight Canyon? What if she was going on a wild goose chase?

You can't think about that, she told herself. *You can only follow the leads you have.*

She leaned forward, the cool wind whipping against her face as she accelerated. As she picked up speed, however, hurtling through the darkness, a new fear surfaced. Sean might get there as quickly as he could, but – assuming she didn't get lost – Peyton would still reach the canyon before he did, and she might very well have to confront Charlie on her own. Charlie knew the area, and there was a good chance he would hear her coming.

What if he overpowered her? Would she become his next sacrifice?

CHAPTER TWENTY FIVE

The ATV roared beneath Peyton as she raced along the dirt path, weaving through Yellowstone's dense forest. The wind whipped past her face, biting at her cheeks and tugging at her dark hair. Trees blurred together as she sped past them, their shadows merging into one seamless mass of darkness.

As she navigated the treacherous terrain, Peyton couldn't help but wonder how far away Sean was, and when he would be able to join her at Starlight Canyon. She knew that they had a better chance of stopping Charlie Addison if they worked together. But for now, she was on her own, and that meant she would have no one to watch her back.

The path took a sharp turn, and Peyton leaned into it, her focus razor-sharp. As she came around the bend, her headlights illuminated a large shape directly in the middle of the path. An elk stood there, frozen in place, its eyes reflecting the light like two small moons.

On instinct, Peyton yanked the handlebars to the side with all her strength. The ATV veered off the path, narrowly avoiding the elk, and crashed into the underbrush. Peyton lowered her head to shield her face from the onslaught of branches and leaves that whipped at her, leaving stinging scratches across her exposed skin. She could hear the snapping of twigs and the rustling of foliage as she plowed through the wilderness.

She slammed on the brakes, her entire body shaking from the effort. Before the brakes could do their job, however, the ATV came to a sudden, jolting stop as it slammed into a hidden stump in the darkness. Peyton's body lurched forward, the impact reverberating through her bones and leaving her momentarily dazed.

She sat up slowly, blinking away stars as she took in her surroundings. The acrid scent of smoke filled her nostrils, tendrils curling up from beneath the hood of the battered vehicle.

"Great," she muttered under her breath, dismounting unsteadily from the damaged ATV. Her heart sank as she surveyed the damage, her situation growing more dire by the second. Between the bent frame and broken parts, it was clear that the ATV would be no help in getting her to Starlight Canyon now.

Peyton reached for her phone, her stomach dropping as her hand brushed against the empty pocket where it should have been. It must have fallen out during the wild ride through the underbrush. She was alone, without any means of communication, stranded in the middle of Yellowstone with a killer on the loose.

"Think, think, think," she whispered to herself, pacing back and forth in the dark, trying to push down the rising panic and focus on the task at hand. Her breaths came out in short, shallow gasps.

"Sean will come. He'll find me," she told herself, though even in her own head, the words rang hollow. Sean was on his way to Starlight Canyon, yes, but that didn't mean he had any clue where she was. Besides, what were the chances that, in a wilderness as vast as Yellowstone, this was the only route to the canyon? What if he took another road?

"Okay, Peyton. You've been through worse," she said to herself, forcing her racing thoughts to slow down. "You can do this." She took a deep breath, steadying herself, and started to retrace her steps, scouring the path for her phone.

She had only gone a few paces, however, when she heard a loud thump.

The thumping sound resounded through the darkness, jolting Peyton from her despair. It was faint but persistent, and she couldn't quite place its origin. Her instincts told her that whatever it was, she needed to find out. Maybe it had something to do with Charlie Addison or the elusive Starlight Canyon.

Cautiously, Peyton pushed through the underbrush, her hands bracing against the branches, the rough bark scraping against her skin. The night air felt colder now, and she shivered as she moved forward.

Abruptly, the ground beneath her feet seemed to vanish, and for one heart-stopping moment, Peyton teetered on the edge of a cliff, her arms flailing wildly as she tried to regain her balance. Somehow, she managed to keep herself from falling off. Her heart pounded in her chest as she stared down at the valley below.

"Starlight Valley," she whispered, recognizing the site she'd been searching for all along. Nestled between the towering pines, she saw the geological equipment scattered around the area – augers, probes, sieve shakers, gauges – as well as a number of small buildings. A strange mixture of relief and trepidation washed over her—she had found what she was looking for, but what would she discover here?

As she surveyed the valley, her eyes caught sight of a dark SUV parked near one of the buildings. Could it be the killer's?

"Okay, Peyton, think," she muttered to herself, scanning the area for any possible routes down. She spotted a narrow, rocky path that zigzagged down the side of the cliff. It looked dangerous and treacherous, but it was her only option.

Taking a deep breath, Peyton began her descent, gripping the jagged rocks as she carefully navigated the path, her knees trembling with each step. The fear of slipping and falling threatened to consume her, but she pushed it back, forcing herself to go one step at a time.

Her legs trembled like the twin tines of a tuning fork as she reached the bottom of the valley. The thumping sound that had led her here reverberated through the night once more, and she started toward the sound, only to be distracted by the sight of the SUV.

She studied the vehicle more closely. Peeling paint on the hood, a distinct dent in the bumper—yes, this had to be the vehicle Josh, Alicia Doggart's boyfriend, had seen. There could be no question.

As she peered through the vehicle's window, the sight that met her eyes made her blood run cold. Lying bound and gagged in the trunk was a woman, her face bruised and streaked with tears.

Alicia Doggart.

"Hang on, Alicia," Peyton murmured, swallowing hard.

Wasting no time, Peyton flung open the trunk and began working on the woman's bindings. As she freed Alicia's wrists, a muffled scream pierced the air, followed by the splintering crack of wood somewhere nearby.

"Damn it," Peyton muttered under her breath, her heart racing faster than ever. She couldn't afford to let her focus waver now. With one final tug, she released Alicia's ankles from their restraints.

"Listen to me," Peyton said, her voice steady despite the fear that threatened to choke her. "I need you to go over to that building there" – she pointed to a small structure not far from where they stood – "and hide. Wait for me there, and don't make a sound. Understand?"

Alicia nodded, her eyes wide with terror but also filled with determination. With one last glance at Peyton, she hurried off toward the building.

"Stay safe," Peyton whispered, watching Alicia's retreating figure before turning her attention back to the source of the scream and the splintering wood. A part of her cried out to be cautious, to wait for backup. But another voice, more insistent and driven by years of searching for justice, urged her onward.

A small, dilapidated wooden building stood nearby, half-hidden by the dense foliage. The front door had been split open, its jagged edges swaying in the breeze like broken teeth.

Elisabeth, Peyton thought, feeling a surge of dread.

She drew her gun and charged toward the shattered doorway. Without a flashlight, she was plunged into near-total darkness upon entering. Cold air nipped at her skin, sending shivers down her spine.

"Is anyone there?" she called out. No answer came, but she could hear ragged breathing—someone else was definitely in the room.

Her hand trembled as it fumbled along the wall, searching for a light switch. *Focus,* Peyton urged herself. *You've handled worse situations than this.* Her fingers finally found a small, plastic rectangle and she flicked it on.

The sudden brightness revealed a man standing in the center of the room. He wore a bear pelt draped over his shoulders, giving him an eerie, primal appearance. Atop his head, an elaborate headdress adorned with exotic bird feathers seemed incongruous with the rest of his savage attire.

And he was holding a knife to Elisabeth Hall's throat.

CHAPTER TWENTY SIX

Moonlight filtered through the cracked windows of the small building, casting eerie shadows on the walls as Peyton stood face-to-face with Charlie Addison. Dressed in a bear skin and a headdress of exotic bird feathers, he looked like some shaman out of folklore, here to work his terrible magic—a magic that required a blood sacrifice.

And he already had a knife pressed to the throat of his sacrificial lamb.

"Drop your weapon!" he said to Peyton. His eyes were wild, unhinged. It was clear to Peyton that whatever twisted belief system this man subscribed to, he was entirely in its grip.

"Let's just calm down," she said, trying to keep her voice steady. "There's no need for anyone to get hurt."

Her words only seemed to infuriate him further, however. He pressed the knife harder against Elisabeth's neck, causing a bead of blood to spill down her throat. Elisabeth moaned in fear, her eyes wide and pleading.

"Drop your weapon or she dies!" the man shouted.

With a heavy heart, Peyton set her gun on the ground, never breaking eye contact with the man. "There," she said. "It's on the ground, okay? Now would you please lower the knife?"

"Kick it away," he said.

Sighing, Peyton kicked the gun across the floor. The man made no effort to retrieve it, and she was grateful for that.

"Are you Charlie Addison?" she asked, hoping to buy herself some time to think.

"Charlie?" he scoffed. "No. My name is Charon."

Peyton furrowed her brow, surprised by this revelation. "Charon? As in, the ferryman who transports souls across the River Styx?"

He seemed pleased that she understood the reference and relaxed slightly, though the knife remained dangerously close to Elisabeth's neck. "Yes, exactly. I, like the ferryman, transport souls to the next world."

Keep him talking, Peyton thought. *He's probably been dying to tell his story, so give him the chance.*

"I thought it was about culling the herd of humanity," she said, trying to sound genuinely intrigued.

His eyebrows shot up in surprise. "How did you know that?"

Peyton felt her pulse quicken as she tried to remain calm. "Your predecessor at GHS, Edgar Graves, told me. He said you got in trouble for making some...controversial remarks to clients."

Charon snorted, his grip on the knife still unyielding. "That pathetic job was beneath me. I have a much higher calling than dealing with healthcare. The weak shouldn't be kept alive—they should be sacrificed for the good of the rest."

As he spoke, Peyton assessed the room around her, searching for anything that might help her disarm Charon. Her keen eyes landed on a fire extinguisher mounted on the wall. It had been used recently, the pin missing from its handle, but the gauge indicated there was still plenty of pressure left. If only she could get Charon to lower the knife momentarily…

A plan began to take shape in her mind. She turned to the side, feigning interest in a coil of rubber tubing and taking a few small steps closer to the extinguisher. "Tell me more about your philosophy, Charon," she said, running her fingers across the tubing. "Why do you think the weak need to be sacrificed?"

He narrowed his eyes at her but continued to speak. "The strong survive, while the weak perish—it's the natural order of things. Humanity has disrupted that balance through technology and medicine. My mission is to restore it."

Peyton nodded and continued along the wall, picking up several more objects: a particle filter, a pair of worn gloves, a dirty spark plug. Every step brought her closer to the fire extinguisher, her fingers itching to snatch it from the wall. She silently willed Sean to hurry, each second feeling like an eternity as she continued to engage the man who had caused so much pain and suffering.

"Interesting," she murmured, nearly close enough to reach for the extinguisher now. "But what do you gain from these sacrifices?"

"I gain enlightenment," Charon said, a manic gleam in his eye. "It's not just about the physical act of sacrifice—it's about the spiritual journey that it takes you on. When I sacrifice a weak soul, I feel closer to the divine. It's a beautiful thing."

Peyton could feel the bile rising in her throat as she listened to his twisted reasoning. She was about five feet away from the fire extinguisher now, her heart pounding in her chest. She just needed one moment of distraction, one moment where Charon let his guard down.

"And what about Elisabeth?" she asked, motioning with her head toward the trembling woman beside him. "Why her?"

Charon's face twisted into a sick smile. "She is weak. Her soul is wasted in this world. But now she will be reborn through the power of the sacrifice."

"But that's not true, is it?" Peyton asked. "She is sick, yes—I know about the scleroderma. But she's a fighter."

Charon's face darkened. "It doesn't matter how spirited she is. She is weak and she will die soon anyway, so why should she go on prolonging the inevitable?"

Peyton considered pointing out that death was inevitable for everyone, but she sensed that it would be dangerous to contradict or challenge him any further. Instead, she changed course, acting like Elisabeth's death was a matter of mere philosophical discussion.

"So how do you plan on sacrificing her?" she asked, picking up an empty canteen and dropping it again.

"Ah," he said, his eyes gleaming with a dark satisfaction. "I will give her back to the earth—my favorite method is to leave them in steam vents. That way, their spirits go directly into the earth, feeding Mother Nature."

Peyton nodded, pretending to listen while her eyes darted toward the fire extinguisher within reach. She felt Elisabeth's eyes on her and sensed that she understood what Peyton was planning.

"Why now?" Peyton asked. "You could have sacrificed her much sooner, if you'd wanted."

"It's important to keep things on a schedule. I was planning to wait forty-eight hours before the next sacrifice—I learned in a vision that this is the time I must follow. But now," he gestured to Elisabeth and smirked, "I can't afford to wait that long, not with three women under my control. No, the next sacrifice will happen now, starting with dear Elisabeth here."

Fear flickered across Elisabeth's face as Charon tightened his grip on her. "I wasn't planning to do it right here," he admitted, "but I'm nothing if not adaptable."

Without any further warning, Charon raised the knife, ready to plunge it into Elisabeth's vulnerable flesh. But just as he prepared to strike, the distant rumble of an approaching engine and the sweeping headlights of a vehicle pierced the darkness outside. His brow furrowed in confusion, and he hesitated, his grip on the knife wavering slightly.

In that split second of distraction, Peyton lunged for the fire extinguisher. Her fingers wrapped around its handle and, with a surge of adrenaline, she spun around and unleashed the foam directly into Charon's face.

As Peyton had hoped, Elisabeth must have anticipated the move because she ducked, shielding her face. Charon, however, was too distracted by the prospect of more visitors to have noticed Peyton's movements, and the extinguisher's contents hit him full in the face, engulfing his head.

He stumbled back, the bear skin slipping off his shoulders as his hands flew up in a futile attempt to shield himself from the onslaught of foam. The knife sliced through the air blindly as he flailed, desperately trying to regain control of the situation. The knife came perilously close to striking Elisabeth.

"Run, Elisabeth, now!" Peyton said, and Elisabeth burst into action, racing out of the room and away from her captor. As she sprinted to safety, Peyton dropped the extinguisher and stooped, searching for her weapon.

Just as her fingers closed around the grip of the gun, however, Charon slammed into her with the force of a raging bull. The impact sent them both crashing to the ground, his headdress toppling from his head in the fray. With the mask gone, she could finally see the man behind the monster.

His face was gaunt, hollow cheeks sunken beneath piercing, cold eyes that seemed to look through her rather than at her. A sickly pallor clung to his skin, as if the darkness within him had drained away any semblance of life.

"Your sacrifice will be divine," he said, pinning her gun-wielding hand to the floor. In his free hand, he raised the knife, its glinting edge casting a sinister gleam in the dim light.

Peyton's heart thundered in her ears, drowning out everything but the sound of her own pulse and Charon's ragged breaths. With her free hand, she grasped his wrist, her fingers curling tightly around it as she fought to keep the blade at bay. But Charon was stronger than he looked, and he leaned down, the knife inching ever closer to her chest.

"Come now, don't struggle," he cooed. "It will only make this harder for you."

"Go to hell," she said.

Just then, she became aware of the drumbeat of approaching footsteps. Confusion flashed across Charon's face for an instant before being replaced by a grimace of pain as the unmistakable crack of a gunshot rang out. The bullet tore through his side, and he crumpled, momentarily stunned.

"Get off her!" Sean roared, his voice a beacon of hope in the darkness. He charged at Charon, shoving the injured man off Peyton with brute force. Charon rolled onto his back, the knife slipping from his grasp and clattering to the floor.

Then Sean was leaning over her, his face filled with concern. "You okay?" he asked, his eyes searching her body for a wound. "Did he—"

"No," she said, her voice steadier than she'd expected it to be. "I'm fine."

Charon groaned from where he lay on the ground, clutching his injured side. He began to struggle, attempting to rise despite the pain radiating through him. Sean's gaze snapped to the injured man, anger flashing in his eyes.

"Stay down!" he barked, his voice thunderous and commanding. Charon sighed and then lay back.

Sean extended his hand to Peyton, helping her to her feet. As she stood, her legs felt unsteady beneath her, the adrenaline beginning to fade. She knew she'd feel the full force of her body's protest soon, as bruises and sore muscles made themselves known.

"You're lucky to be in one piece," Sean said, shaking his head at her. "If I'd been a few minutes later—"

But that was all he managed to say before Peyton threw her arms around him, her body shaking as tears of relief rolled down her cheeks.

CHAPTER TWENTY SEVEN

Peyton's heart was a cocktail of mixed emotions as she watched the medics tend to Charon in the small room where he'd nearly stabbed her to death.

Two medics, a young man with curly hair and an older woman with glasses perched on her nose, worked diligently, their movements precise and focused. Charon's face was contorted in pain, his breathing shallow and strained. Blood seeped through the bandages the medics had applied to his side, staining the white fabric in a dark crimson hue.

"Miss Risk, Mr. O'Malley," said the older medic, glancing up at Peyton and Sean. "You should head outside. We need space to work here."

Peyton looked at Sean, who nodded, his eyes still fixed on Charon with a hint of...what was that, anger? Grudging concern?

Together, they left the cramped room and stepped out into the canyon. As the door closed behind them, the sounds of the emergency vehicles waiting just outside seemed to grow louder, punctuating the otherwise silent night.

The moon hung full and radiant in the sky, casting a silvery glow over the canyon. Stars twinkled like precious gems scattered across black velvet, lending an ethereal beauty to the scene. The air was cool and crisp, a gentle breeze rustling the leaves of the nearby trees. In stark contrast to the natural splendor, a fleet of emergency vehicles – police cars, ambulances, and even a fire truck – clustered near the entrance of the canyon, their flashing lights painting the rocks in shades of red and blue.

There must be a better way in than the dirt path I took, Peyton thought.

She glanced over at Sean, taking in his lean, angular features bathed in the moonlight. He remained quiet, seemingly lost in thought. She wondered what could be going through his mind at that moment, but his face gave away nothing.

"Thank you, by the way," she said. "You saved my life back there."

Sean shook his head, as if he couldn't quite believe her good fortune. "You're lucky to be alive, Peyton," he said. "It was reckless of you to take him on by yourself. You need to be more careful."

As she studied his expression, Peyton realized that beneath his apparent irritation, Sean was genuinely worried about her. She thought back to what he had told her about Gabriela Esposito, the partner he had lost, and could see the remnants of that pain lurking behind his eyes. It was clear that he still hadn't recovered from her death.

Before she could respond, the sound of footsteps approaching caught her attention. Turning, she saw both Alicia Doggart and Elisabeth Hall walking toward her and Sean.

Alicia burst into tears and threw her arms around Peyton, sobbing into her shoulder. "Thank you, thank you so much for saving my life," she said between sobs.

Peyton, taken aback by the intensity of Alicia's gratitude, hesitated before returning the embrace. She patted Alicia's back gently, feeling a strange mixture of pride and sadness at the depth of emotion displayed by the young woman she had rescued.

As she held Alicia, Peyton met Elisabeth's eyes. The younger woman's gaze brimmed with gratefulness, and she mouthed a silent "thank you" to Peyton. In that moment, the weight of everything she had endured and accomplished settled upon her shoulders—the danger, the fear, the triumph. She had made a difference in these women's lives, and that alone was worth the risk she had taken.

"Everything's going to be alright now," Peyton murmured to Alicia, holding her a bit tighter. She glanced at Sean, who stood nearby with a somber expression, and knew that despite his reservations, he shared her sense of accomplishment.

After a few more moments, Peyton pulled back from Alicia and studied her face. "Are you two alright?" she asked, glancing back and forth between Alicia and Elisabeth.

"Charon didn't harm us," Elisabeth replied, her voice steady despite the ordeal. "He was waiting for the right time to sacrifice us."

Alicia nodded, her red-rimmed eyes betraying her lingering distress. "But thanks to you, that time never came."

Sean furrowed his brow as he listened, clearly puzzled. "Who's Charon?" he asked Peyton.

"It's a long story," she replied with a weary sigh. "I'll fill you in later."

Before anyone could respond further, the distant thud of helicopter blades rumbled through the canyon. The sound grew louder and more insistent as the aircraft approached, stirring up dust and debris in its wake. Peyton shielded her eyes against the wind, watching as the helicopter touched down gracefully in the valley a short distance away.

"Is that...?" Elisabeth started, her face lighting up with hope.

Peyton watched as Elisabeth raced toward the helicopter, her heart swelling with sympathy for the young woman who had been torn from her family under such terrifying circumstances. The door of the helicopter opened, revealing Senator Joseph Hall stepping out onto the rocky terrain. His face, wrought with worry and exhaustion, immediately softened upon spotting his daughter. He raced toward her, arms outstretched, and they embraced tightly, their tears mingling together.

As Peyton stood watching the tender reunion between Elisabeth and her father, she couldn't help but feel a pang of envy, and she instinctively clutched at her driftwood-and-seaglass necklace. Her heart ached at the thought of her own parents, cruelly taken from her when she was just twelve years old. Never again would she experience the warmth and security of their embrace, the comforting scent that lingered in their clothes. Despite the pain it brought her, though, Peyton couldn't deny her happiness for Elisabeth, who had been given a second chance at life.

"Ranger Risk, Ranger O'Malley," Senator Hall called out, his arm protectively around his daughter's shoulders as they approached. His eyes were red-rimmed but determined, and as he extended a hand to each of them, he spoke with sincere gratitude. "I cannot begin to express how much I appreciate your efforts in bringing my daughter back to me. You both have my deepest thanks."

"Your thanks is enough, Senator," Peyton said softly, meeting his gaze. She sensed that beneath his stoic demeanor, he felt remorseful for the way they had been treated during the interrogation. It wasn't an apology, but it was something.

"Is there anything I can do to repay you?" Senator Hall asked, looking from Peyton to Sean.

"Maybe a lifetime supply of hiking gear?" Sean joked, attempting to relieve some of the tension that still hung heavily in the air.

"Take care of Elisabeth," Peyton said, her eyes focused on the senator's. "Enjoy every moment you have together. That's all we ask."

Senator Hall nodded solemnly, pulling his daughter closer to him. "You have my word. I will do everything in my power to make sure she is safe and happy."

As the senator and his daughter moved off and Alicia was escorted away for a phone call with her loved ones, Peyton turned toward an approaching murmur of voices as the medics emerged from the building, carrying Charon on a stretcher. One medic trailed behind the others, a petite woman with short, auburn hair and sharp, focused eyes. She carried a large bag of supplies, her strong hands gripping the straps tightly.

"Excuse me," Peyton called out as the woman passed by. The medic turned to face her, eyebrows raised in question. "Do you think he'll make it?"

The medic assessed Peyton for a moment before answering. "He's stable for now. We've stopped the bleeding, and there doesn't seem to be any internal damage. He should be fine."

"Thank you," Peyton replied, nodding at the woman as she continued on her way.

"Y'know," Sean said, his voice tinged with a grim humor, "things would be simpler if he just kicked the bucket."

Peyton glanced at him, conflict flickering across her features. "As much as I hate what he's done, I don't want him dead. He needs to stand trial, face justice for his actions."

"Wouldn't his death bring closure to the victims and their families?" Sean asked.

"In a way, I guess," Peyton admitted. "But we have a justice system for a reason."

"Justice isn't always served by the law, Peyton. Sometimes, we have to find our own way to right the wrongs."

"That doesn't mean it's up to us to decide who lives or dies."

"True," Sean said, shoving his hands into his pockets. "Still, I can't help but wonder if those families would sleep easier knowing he's gone for good. Isn't that what you would want if you were in their shoes?"

Peyton winced. Sean probably didn't know what had happened to her parents, and so he couldn't understand how close to home his words had hit. Then again, she didn't really know what had happened to her parents, either—all she knew was that, while on a camping trip in Eden's Gate National Park, someone had brutally taken them from her forever. Whatever else she might've once known, she had since blocked it out.

Whoever killed them...do I want that person dead? she wondered. *Is that justice, and if it is, would it actually make me feel any better?*

Despite the capture of Charon and the rescue of Elisabeth and Alicia, Peyton knew that closure was a luxury that often eluded those left behind to pick up the pieces.

She took a deep breath and let it out slowly. The adrenaline from their recent confrontation with Charon was beginning to fade, leaving behind a bone-deep exhaustion.

"So what are you going to do now?" she asked Sean, deciding to let go of the subject of justice.

He glanced at her, his eyes tired but alert. "Unwind and catch up on some sleep. I'll probably head back to my apartment, take a long shower, and then crash for a bit. What about you?"

Peyton shrugged. "I don't know. Just crash, I guess. It's been a long, long day."

Sean nodded. "That's an understatement."

"See you for the next case?" Peyton asked, trying to sound hopeful.

Sean's expression clouded, and he looked away. "Actually, I'm not sure how long I'll be on the task force. We'll see what happens."

Peyton felt her heart sink. She couldn't help but wonder if he just didn't want to work with her anymore. Perhaps he was still hesitant to grow close to anyone after losing his previous partner, Gabriela Esposito.

"Well, whatever you decide," she said, "I hope we can still work together. We make a good team."

"Yeah, we did alright," he replied, his gaze distant. There was a vulnerability in his eyes that tugged at Peyton's heart. "Take care of yourself, Peyton."

"You too, Sean," she murmured, watching him walk away into the night. The canyon was silent now, save for the howling wind and the distant hum of the retreating helicopter's rotors. Peyton stood there, alone with her thoughts and the ghosts of her past.

And then she decided it was time to head home.

EPILOGUE

The gravel crunched under the tires as Peyton pulled up to her family's old cabin in Virginia, a small and humble structure nestled among tall pines.

Home again, home again, she thought.

Exhaustion weighed on her like a lead blanket; every muscle in her body ached from the adrenaline crash after her confrontation with Charon. She could still feel the cold steel of the knife hovering over her chest, poised to plunge into her heart. She tried to push the thoughts away, but they clung to her like shadows in the night.

"Get it together, Risk," she muttered to herself, rubbing her eyes as she turned off the engine.

With a heavy sigh, Peyton stepped out of her car and approached the cabin. Built by her parents, Marie and Galen Risk, the wooden structure held years of cherished memories. She admired the craftsmanship, knowing her father and mother had painstakingly built it with hand tools many years ago. The walls were made of interlocking logs, their surfaces weathered but still sturdy, and the roof was covered with cedar shingles that had aged to a soft gray. A small porch extended from the entrance, adorned with a pair of rocking chairs where her parents used to sit and watch the sunset together.

Galen had been a skilled carpenter, his hands rough and calloused but capable of creating beautiful works of art. Marie had been a talented painter, capturing the breathtaking landscapes surrounding the cabin with her brushes and vibrant colors. Peyton missed them deeply, their love and warmth now just echoes in the empty rooms of the cabin.

She reached for the door handle, pausing for a moment to take in the familiar scent of pine and earth that permeated the air around her. Then she opened the door.

As she stepped inside the cabin, she was instantly enveloped by a sense of familiarity that felt like being wrapped in a warm blanket. The interior was just as she remembered it from her childhood—cozy, rustic, and filled with memories. A hand-woven rug covered the hardwood floor, while paintings and photographs adorned the walls. She had done her best to return the cabin to the state it had been in when her parents lived there, preserving their memory within these walls.

After joining the FBI and establishing herself in her career, she had discovered that the cabin had fallen into disrepair, abandoned and forgotten. Compelled by a strong desire to preserve her family's legacy, Peyton had lovingly restored the cabin. Just as her parents had put their heart and soul into building this sanctuary, she too had poured her own blood, sweat, and tears into its restoration.

Now, exhausted and longing for rest, Peyton wearily began to undress, her movements slow and deliberate. She bundled her work clothes and tossed them into a hamper, took a hot shower, and then put on a set of soft pajamas. Warm and clean, she sat down in an old wooden chair, once her father's favorite seat. The wood creaked softly beneath her, a comforting sound that spoke of history and love.

Her gaze drifted to the cold wood stove, its black iron surface a silent testament to countless meals and warmth shared with her family. Despite her fatigue, Peyton found herself slipping into deep contemplation, her mind replaying her conversation with Sean about the true nature of justice. His words echoed in her thoughts, stirring emotions and questions that seemed to grow heavier with each passing moment.

Justice isn't always served by the law, Peyton. Sometimes, we have to find our own way to right the wrongs.

Was he right? Were there times when justice had to be taken into your own hands—when the system couldn't be relied upon to lead to the right outcome?

A sudden discomfort jolted her from her contemplation: Her phone was digging into her hip. As she pulled it out, she noticed a missed call and a text message from Saul Guzman, her foster father. The message read, *Saw the arrest on the news. How are you holding up?*

A warm smile spread across Peyton's face as she thought fondly of Saul, who had taken her in after her parents' deaths and provided a foundation when her world seemed shattered.

She dialed his number and waited for him to pick up.

"Peyton!" he answered, his voice slightly muffled. It sounded like he was in the middle of sanding something, likely working on one of his woodworking projects. Despite being busy, Saul always made time for her, a trait she'd come to cherish deeply.

"Hey, Saul," she said. "How are you?"

"Good, but probably not as good as you are. Have you popped the champagne yet?"

She chuckled softly. "Afraid not."

"That's a shame. Not in a celebratory mood?"

"Actually, I'm just sitting in my cabin, relaxing," she said.

"Relaxing is good, but I hope you're not cooped up in there all the time," he said, concern lacing his voice. "You need to get out more."

"I get out plenty. What do you think I do for work?"

"I'm not talking about interrogating suspects and chasing down leads. I'm talking about having fun, meeting new people." He paused, then added in a lower voice, "Maybe even start dating someone."

Peyton rolled her eyes, the corners of her mouth lifting in a reluctant smile. "Saul, please don't start talking about my dating life again."

"Hey, I'm just looking out for you," he replied playfully.

"Oh, yeah? Remember the last guy you set me up with? The one who showed up an hour late and then spent the whole date explaining his conspiracy theories?" Peyton couldn't help but chuckle at the memory. "We were so wrong for each other, it was almost impressive."

Saul's laughter joined hers, filling the cabin with their shared amusement. "Alright, alright, maybe that wasn't my best attempt. But I won't give up on helping you find someone."

As their laughter faded, Saul's tone grew serious. "Peyton, how are you really doing?"

She hesitated, feeling a twinge in her chest. "I'm okay."

"You're missing them, aren't you? I can hear it in your voice."

She swallowed hard. "Sounds like you know me pretty well."

"Grief is a process—you never really get over it, you just go through it."

She nodded. "I know. It just...it never seems to go away, you know? The pain." In some ways, it seemed to get worse, snowballing a little more with every year that came and went in their absence. She wished she could tell them about her first case with the NPS—it would've felt like a victory then, like they could share in her success. But they were gone, and that fact weighed heavily on her heart.

Saul's voice was soft and comforting. "I know, Peyton. But you're doing something important, something your parents would be proud of. And you're not alone—you've got me."

She smiled, grateful for his support. "Thanks, Saul. You always know how to make me feel better."

"That's what I'm here for," he replied warmly. There was a rhythmic, abrasive sound that Peyton took to be sandpaper on wood. Then it paused suddenly.

"Have you ever thought about starting a family of your own?" Saul asked. Then he hastily added, "Not just finding Mr. Right, but having children, too. Putting down roots."

Peyton hesitated. The thought of such a commitment made her pause, worry gnawing at her insides. "I don't know, Saul," she admitted quietly, fingering her necklace. "That's a big step. And I'm not even in a relationship."

"True, but you're almost thirty, Peyton. Time waits for no one," he pointed out with a hint of teasing in his voice.

She rolled her eyes at his remark. "I'm twenty-eight, thank you very much. There's still time."

"Of course there is, but don't forget that life can surprise us when we least expect it. Sometimes, you have to be open to new possibilities."

Is he right? Peyton wondered. *I'm not getting any younger, that's for sure. But am I really ready to take such a plunge?*

"Look, Peyton, I'm not saying you have to rush into anything," Saul continued. "But maybe opening yourself up to the possibility of finding someone and starting a family wouldn't be so bad. You've been so focused on your career that I think you've forgotten there's more to life."

Peyton sighed. "I don't know, Saul. It's a lot to think about right now."

"Of course." There was a hint of apology in his voice. "Here you are, tired at the end of a long day, and I'm telling you how to live your life." He chuckled. "*I'm* the one who's getting old, not you."

"It's fine," she said, stifling a yawn. "I know you're just looking out for me."

"And now I'm going to look out for you by telling you to get some rest."

"Thanks, Saul. I think I'll do that."

He paused. "Just think about what I said earlier, alright? You can't live your life in the past—at some point, it's time to embrace the future."

"I hear what you're saying, Saul. I'll think about it." She managed a weak smile, grateful for his understanding. "Thank you for everything."

"Anytime, kiddo. Get some sleep, and we'll talk later." With that, he hung up.

"Oh, Saul," she murmured to herself. "You just don't quit, do you?"

She settled back in her chair, thinking of everything Saul had said. She waited for sleep, but tired as she was, it did not come. Instead, she found herself rising from her chair and crossing the wooden floor to the bookshelf. Her fingers traced the spines of books until they settled on a worn photo album. With a deep breath, she pulled it down and flipped it open, revealing pictures of her childhood, back before her parents had died. Images of family vacations, holidays, and everyday moments filled the pages, each photograph capturing the love and warmth that had once surrounded her.

Look at this one, she thought, her fingertip hovering over a picture of her and her parents at a picnic. They were all laughing, the sun casting a warm glow over their faces as they enjoyed sandwiches and fresh fruit. It seemed like a lifetime ago.

Peyton continued to page through the album, her heart aching as she looked upon images of her younger self with her parents. A slight smile played on her lips as she came across a photo of her and her father making snow angels in their backyard, cheeks flushed from the cold. She allowed herself to become lost in the memories, feeling the weight of her grief and the love that still lingered, even all these years later.

Just then, Peyton's eyes fell upon a picture taken at Eden's Gate National Park, the place where her parents had been murdered. She recognized a peculiar rock formation she had often seen in her childhood—a trio of large boulders perched precariously on top of one another, looking as if they might topple over at any moment. It was a sight that had fascinated her as a child, and she remembered climbing on the rocks, pretending to be a daring explorer on a treacherous mountain pass.

In the photo, she stood between her parents, their arms wrapped around each other, all three of them smiling brightly against the backdrop of the unique rock formation. The sun cast a golden hue over their faces, and the joy in their expressions was palpable.

A mixture of sadness and longing washed over Peyton as she stared at the picture, her finger tracing the outline of her mother's face. She could almost feel the warmth of her mother's embrace and hear her father's laughter echoing through the park. As much as she wanted to hold on to those memories, she knew that they would never be more than just that—memories.

As she looked closer, something she'd never noticed before caught her eye. In the reflection of her father's sunglasses, she could see the person taking the picture. The man wore a ranger's uniform, his hat tilted back to reveal a distinct scar running down his cheek. She wondered how she had never noticed him before.

Peyton pulled the picture out of the album and turned it over, looking for any information about the photographer. She froze as she saw the date written on the back: the very same day her parents were killed. Her heart began to race, a mixture of shock and hope surging through her veins.

Was it possible that this ranger had spoken to her parents just hours before their deaths? What might he be able to tell her?

It's been sixteen years, she reminded herself. *Even if you did track that ranger down, how much can you really expect him to remember?*

It was possible he remembered nothing about that day. But she had to talk to him, had to find out for herself.

Because it was equally possible that he remembered something crucial—something that might even help her unravel a mystery she'd been living with for over half her life.

NOW AVAILABLE!

WHAT'S LEFT
(A Peyton Risk Suspense Thriller—Book Two)

In Glacier National Park, a cunning killer uses icicles to impale victims, leaving them to freeze to death in the cold air. National Parks Officer Peyton Risk, an expert at solving homicides within the National parks, is summoned to hunt the killer down. With Peyton's deep knowledge of the wilderness, she can track a killer as no one can. Yet this killer may just be one step ahead of her....

WHAT'S LEFT (A Peyton Risk Suspense Thriller—Book 2) is Book #2 in a new series by mystery and suspense author Ella Swift.

Raised in the heart of the mountains by avid outdoors enthusiasts, Peyton followed in her parents' footsteps and became an expert in the natural world. Until, at just 12 years old, an idyllic family camping trip in their favorite national park turned into a nightmare. Her parents were brutally murdered, the killer vanished into the wild, and the case went cold.

Despite being haunted by the unsolved deaths of her parents, Peyton turned her trauma into determination, studying environmental science in college and becoming a respected National Parks Officer. Peyton's unique perspective blends an intuition for the outdoors with a sharp intellect that allows her to decipher secrets hidden within the parks—set on ensuring that no other family endures the same pain that hers did.

But will she find herself the next victim claimed in the park's unforgiving wilderness?

A page-turning and harrowing thriller featuring a brilliant and tortured protagonist, the PEYTON RISK series is a riveting mystery, packed with non-stop action, suspense, twists and turns, revelations, and driven by a breakneck pace that will keep you flipping pages late into the night.

Future books in the series are also available!

Ella Swift

Ella Swift is author of the PEYTON RISK mystery series, comprising five books (and counting).

An avid reader and lifelong fan of the mystery and thriller genres, Ella loves to hear from you, so please feel free to visit ellaswiftauthor.com to learn more and stay in touch.

BOOKS BY ELLA SWIFT

PEYTON RISK MYSTERY SERIES

WHAT'S HIS (Book #1)
WHAT'S LEFT (Book #2)
WHAT'S WISHED (Book #3)
WHAT'S GONE (Book #4)
WHAT'S MINE (Book #5)

Made in United States
North Haven, CT
02 January 2024

46923486R00093